THE GIRL
in the
TIME MACHINE
by
Debra Chapoton

This is a work of fiction. Names, characters, places, and incidents either are the product of the author's imagination or are used fictitiously.

Cover art by Boone Patchard

ISBN-10 : 1523967552
ISBN-13 : 978-1523967551

Debra Chapoton

Novels by Debra Chapoton

Edge of Escape

The Guardian's Diary

Sheltered

A Soul's Kiss

Exodia

Out of Exodia

The Time Bender

The Time Pacer

The Time Stopper

The Time Ender

The Girl in the Time Machine

To Die Upon a Kiss

Here Without a Trace

Love Contained

Spell of the Shadow Dragon

Chapter 1

What did we (two nervous, frantic girls) do with a dead body while a storm brewed outside, the lights actually flickered, and the minutes ticked closer to the moment when my car would drive up—with me driving? You would have thought we'd discussed the subject before. Because in less than five minutes of rational, scientific debate we settled on burying Megan, time machine style, in the hill out back. It sounded cold and callous, but really it was the best thing for everyone.

Mack made agitated chimpanzee howls when we dragged Megan down the hall, past his cell. The steps were the worst. Her toes smacked every stair tread with a dull thump. It was heartbreaking.

***

I hope you're reading this, Skylar. Or Emily. Or whatever you're calling yourself in your new reality. (I'm still going by Laken Mitchell, by the way.)

Sorry.

Sorry about leaving you in the past. I'm writing this down—a totally complete explanation and apology—so you'll understand. And so when, and if, we meet up again in some future or past you'll have already forgiven me.

Unfortunately, I'm pretty sure we'll never be best friends again where I am now. Never finish high school together. Never have another sleep over where we dye my hair black and bleach yours blond. Never giggle over you-know-who's cute butt.

1

Never.

Anybody who did what I did—what we did—would eventually lose someone. Kill someone. Accidentally … or not so accidentally. And sometimes you can see death on someone's face. There's nothing you can do then except move on. Right? Right?

I'm going to leave this diary at the pump house in hopes you'll find it. That seems to be the only place that didn't change. I can only hope that maybe an earlier version of you or me will find it, read it, and figure out a way to restore things. After all, I seem to be getting smarter with every time jump. It's the hibernation that's the killer.

Anyway, I'll just record everything in this journal the way I remember it. Here goes:

On a sunny Saturday morning when I was ten—that might be twenty years or so into your future—I went into our garage, hunched over the front fender of my bike, and pressed on pink stickers. My dad came out, pulled his car out into the driveway, and then hummed as he cleared off the top of a small workbench against the back wall. He drilled a hole into a brick and put a bolt through it. I stopped to watch him. He snapped a set of keys onto the end of the bolt and then used a soldering gun to melt the ring closed. After that those four keys weren't going anywhere without the brick.

"Why are you doing that?" I asked. I expected one of his long explanations. Remember how he could hold us spellbound with his scientific descriptions? What a science geek. In a good way. I loved my dad—my real dad, the first and original version of him, that is—and I guess you got to know that version best.

"You'll find out when you're older, Laken." A tight smirk and a raised eyebrow—I knew that look. It meant subject closed.

Picture my dad, that super brainy nerd, with his full professor's beard and that unfortunate bald spot, yeah, picture him giving me that look. I knew better than to nag at him. I went back to working on my bike, rearranging my stickers while he made several more sets of bricks with keys. I never suspected the bricks and keys had anything to do with all the missing girls in our town, even though by then I'd heard loads of tales about kidnappers and serial killers. I told you all about those stories as soon as we met, remember? Who would've thought one day I'd be all those things—kidnapper, missing girl, and killer.

I didn't think much about the bricks and keys until a couple of years later when my parents started dragging me to work with them on weekends and I saw them use the keys on the brick to gain access to their lab. That was around the time I got my first period, right before my birthday, still four years before you moved to town. I'm only writing this part down because what happened then changed my life in the worst and maybe the best way and I don't think I explained it to you before.

Up until then I had a few friends—none as good as you— and I was doing well in middle school. You know me, I never got into trouble. But one day, the day before I turned twelve, trouble found me.

Shelly Ayers—lunchroom loudmouth, smarty-pants, sometimes teacher's pet—passed several notes out, one to each boy in our class. I only know what the notes said because a kid named Lawrence stuck one in my book later; it said *check out Laken Mitchell's butt*. Worst day ever. Bloody jeans, bloody chair, cruel laughter. You get the picture. When I came home from school and begged my mom not to ever make me go back there, she drove me to the lab and asked my dad to show me what was in the tower, locked off by the fourth key on the brick.

Physically I'd become a woman and symbolically my parents acknowledged that by revealing a massively unbelievable secret.

Well, you know what that secret was: they had a time machine in the tower.

For weeks after that I thought of only three things: compassion—why didn't Shelly Ayers have any? Revenge—how could I get mine? And the machine in the tower—how did it work?

Shelly's cruel joke changed my life and I wasn't about to forget it. A part of me wanted nothing better than to "do unto her" in an equally unsympathetic manner, but the horrific humiliation I suffered also produced feelings I recognized much later as empathy. So even though I wanted something awful to happen to her—get run over by a car, drown in her bathtub—I also began at that time to develop a sensitivity to other girls' feelings though I withdrew from my few friendships. What I saw in the tower of the lab tickled my imagination and in the basement of my mind I began to fantasize about how I could use my father's invention for revenge … and for good, too, of course.

On through middle school and into high school there were multiple incidents, other emotional upsets, and humiliations I endured at the hands of bullies and mean girls. They shaped my thinking. And my actions.

The very day I got my driver's license, a Friday, my mom and dad shooed me out the door after dinner, told me to drive solo all over town, and enjoy my new freedom. Visit some friends, they said, go shopping or find a party. Yeah, like that was going to happen. They just didn't want me going with them back to the lab where they worked practically 24/7. I spent too much time training the mice, they said. I shouldn't get so attached, they said. But what else did I have to do? That was before you entered my life. Well, the seventeen-year-old you.

But I didn't argue. I took the car keys and drove everywhere I'd practiced driving before: through town, a short way into the country, a few miles on the expressway, back through town and down some side streets until it started getting dark. I burned through a quarter of a tank of gas without spotting a single "friend" or party or even getting near the mall.

I drove to my high school and then followed the convoluted bus route home, hoping I'd never have to take that route—seated in the spot behind the bus driver—again. It wound through several subdivisions and seemed totally alien to me at night. That's when my headlights caught a wobbly Shelly Ayers on foot. She looked lost. She took a step and stumbled, lurched toward the pavement, then hobbled a little further along somebody's lawn. Could she be drunk? I passed her, pulled into a driveway and reversed direction to come up beside her. I rolled down my window and let my compassionate side take control.

"Shelly? Do you need a ride?"

She staggered to the window and caught her balance with a hand on my door. Her hair swung forward and she used her other hand to tuck a snarly mass of it behind her ear. One of her eyes looked swollen and red and there were scratches on her face from her temple to her chin. The front of her shirt was wet and her breath stank of beer. Yup, she was drunk. But there was something else, something out of place about her.

"A ride?" she said. "You'd give me a ride? But—" She teetered to the side then righted herself and leaned fully on the door, poking her head in through the window, hippie beads jangling. There was no way I could open it then. She reached both arms through the window like she wanted to give me a hug.

Her whole upper body was aiming to follow and I was afraid she'd vomit on my lap next.

I put the car in park and slid across to the passenger side to get out. I went around and guided her to the passenger's door and got her buckled in.

"I can't go home. I can't go home." She sobbed into her hands and kept repeating the refrain.

"Why not?" I turned off the engine and tried not to think how I had my first enemy literally in my clutches. Did I still want revenge? Honestly, Sky, I think I did, but I was trying really hard to be compassionate.

She wiped at her eyes and took a couple of stuttering breaths, like a kid does after she's balled her head off, and then she fumbled with her beads and started singing an old Beatles song. I waited patiently while finally she composed herself and spoke clearly. "My parents abuse me."

I never expected to hear that. "Should we call the police?"

"My step-father is a cop. So … no. Can't call the cops."

"Well, what do you mean they abuse you? Like hit you?"

"That and worse. It's why I drink, why I—" She gulped back a sob. "I can't go home. I never want to go home again." She suddenly seemed almost sober. She pulled at the holes in the knees of her jeans.

"I have an idea. I'm sure my parents will go for it." I smiled at her and continued, "They own a place where you can live. You could be like the night watchman or something. Maybe clean the animal cages in exchange for living there, at their laboratory."

Shelly got real still. Hopeful, I guessed. Yeah, I was doing a good deed. This felt better than revenge. She looked so pathetic.

"You'd really help me?"

"Sure. Let's go talk to them now. They're at the lab."

6

I started the car and drove out of the subdivision. Shelly didn't say another word as I headed straight to Mitchell Labs, where my folks would be, where they always were, where they'd worked together since they bought the land and old buildings.

Shelly gave a startled cry when we hit the first speed bump on the driveway into the lab. It was a long driveway and especially spooky at night.

"Where are you taking me?"

"Don't worry," I said, "this is where my parents work. It's really cool. You'll like it. It's pretty bright inside."

I felt a little disobedient bringing someone to the lab, but only because I'd never done it before. Of course, you already know about how my parents bought an old monastery and remodeled the interior to start Mitchell Labs. They'd done it with money they won right after they graduated from college. You probably also figured out right away why they were super lucky—it took me a while to figure out why—and why even though we were probably millionaires (well duh, you saw the treasure chest), we lived like ordinary middle-class people in that old-style three-bedroom ranch. I didn't want to take Shelly to my house, but the lab would impress her. So what if in the back of my mind I was also thinking about what was in the tower. And maybe a seedling of revenge was taking root over the kind-heartedness I meant to cultivate.

(Wow, Skylar, it feels really good to confess all this to you.)

We traveled down the long twisty road and I expected Shelly to gasp at the specter of the old crumbling monastery, but she had her head down in her hands again and missed seeing me switch to high beams, on and off three times, to signal my arrival—it was what my mom always did when she brought me here at night. I parked close up to the front door instead of going around to the back gated entrance. I didn't have the key, or the brick it was attached to, so knocking on the front tower door would have to work.

Parked there with the headlights aiming off into the woods and only a little light illuminating the stone façade was a lot less intimidating. I beeped the horn three times then went to the door and knocked. It took a few minutes and some extra hard pounding, but finally both my mom and my dad opened the door and looked from me to the bedraggled passenger in the car.

In a harsh whisper my dad scolded me for bringing someone to the lab. "Laken, what were you thinking? You know better." My mom was right beside him shaking her head, a concerned look tightening the lines around her mouth.

"No. Listen. This is Shelly Ayers. She can't go home. I thought she could stay here. Work for you. Live at the lab." I added in an even lower whisper, "She won't find out what's in the tower."

"What? Laken, you know we can't do that."

"But, dad, her parents will kill her, I mean actually kill her, if she goes home. Please, can't she stay here for a while?" I glanced back at Shelly. The dome light was still on and her face looked made up for Halloween, mascara running down, eyes dark, hair matted. I looked back at my parents, made my case outlining a job for her at the lab, how she could sleep in one of the rooms, and ended with "Please?"

Mom stepped forward. "She can spend the night at our house. Take her there. We'll talk in the morning." She pulled on my dad's elbow, stepping back as if to say "end of discussion." Okay, I got it. So much for trying to do a good deed. You'd think they'd be happy I'd found a friend. But no. Their reaction was nothing like when I brought you home.

They closed the door and I got back in the car.

"What did they say?"

I waited a beat. "They said no." Another sigh. "But you can spend the night at my house. We'll figure something out."

She slumped lower in the seat and pulled the seat belt away from her throat. "Might as well drive me off the bridge," she mumbled. It flashed through my mind that a few years ago I had hoped for such an end for her.

I took us home and parked out in the street so my folks could pull in more easily at whatever late hour they finally returned. Shelly needed my help to walk without falling. I encouraged her to take a shower to sober up and I lent her my favorite pajamas. We ate some junk food and started talking.

And talking. She unloaded every sordid detail of a horrible life. I had no idea anyone, anywhere, ever had to endure the awful abuse that she did. I guess I cried as much as she did that night. And I tried to forgive her for what she did to me long ago, though I didn't say so out loud.

My parents came home around midnight and went to bed without checking on us. We kept talking, or rather, Shelly kept talking, telling me about her succession of evil step-fathers. I lost track of how many times her mother had been married or pretended to be. Shelly's real father was in and out of the picture, and he was nothing to brag about either. The one positive was Shelly's interest in music; she could quote a string of lyrics to fit as captions to each scene she described. Scenes of maltreatment, neglect, and injury. I guess the music was her way of coping.

"I wish I was somewhere else. I wish I was some *time* else," she said.

I nodded. I thought of the tower. I thought of what was in the tower.

9

It was rash, it was impulsive, I knew that, but with a sudden increase in my heart rate I had the perfect answer and came to the realization that I was going to totally exploit what was in the tower. For good, a good cause. Not revenge.

"Shelly, if you could live any time, like the turn of the century, or before there were computers, or like the 1950s, what would you choose?"

She didn't think long. "The 1960s. I'd want to be around for the beginning of when music really got cool. The Beatles ..." She went on naming other groups, but I stopped listening because I was planning how we'd sneak through the house, grab one of the bricks with the keys, take the car that was parked on the street, and steal back to the lab where I could make all of Shelly's troubles disappear.

Chapter 2

Destiny has a way of kicking you in the butt even when you're trying to do the right thing. Well, I guess you know that.

I took care of Shelly's problem that night. I watched her leave. I stood there all full of worried expectations and hope ... and I did it. I pulled it off. It was no different than watching white mice get "disappeared" which I'd seen my father do several times. With his usual long-winded explanations my dad had inadvertently taught me how to use the time machine. It was a complicated metal and chrome and steel contraption. The giant structure shined, all sterile and alien and medical with a bit of military green at its base. The bed-like platform where Shelly, and countless mice, had been positioned before their journeys into the past or future now sat empty. I had set the controls, nodded my head and smiled. It was too easy.

I stood next to the computer controls and coped with a moment of regret. What had I done?

There was no way to undo it. There was no way to bring her back.

But I'd saved her. I kept telling myself that. Her disappearance would be written off as a runaway. Nobody saw her get in my car. There was no link to me. My parents never saw her at our house. Who's to say I did or didn't take her home?

I had the brick with the keys. I locked everything up. I drove home and parked in the street, snuck back to my room and slept until noon. My parents never mentioned a word about my bringing her to the lab that night. I wrote that off to their preoccupation with their scientific endeavors.

Three weeks later, when the gossip at school over her disappearance had died down—her mother even told the school she'd gone to live with her grandparents—I started making a list of people, mostly girls, who could benefit from my "help." I kneaded my conscience into acceptance and yielded to my secret power and compulsion. My compassionate action toward Shelly was the first in a series of disappearances. And I felt justified after I did some computer research on Shelly, one of the things I did to ease my conscience. Thankfully she hadn't changed her name and I could follow the line of her life through the miracle of the internet. I took that as confirmation that I had done the right thing. I wouldn't let myself believe that the only Shelly Ayers that came up on Google, a woman who'd reached adulthood in the late 1960s, was anyone other than the frightened, desperate teen I'd gone to school with. She'd survived the time travel and grown up in the past.

I wrote her name at the top of the list of several girls, then crossed it out.

1. ~~Shelly Ayers~~
2. Erica Wills
3. Ciera Nielson
4. Melissa Poznansky
5. Cara Branieki
6. Megan Hodges

It was just coincidence that the girls I listed had wronged me in the past. Okay, I'll admit to you, Sky, that a smidgeon of revenge tainted my efforts, but truly, I only picked girls who needed to get away—ones who were destined to face death or disease or shame if they stayed. I didn't dwell on the fact that they all came from the pool of people who had hurt me.

Life went on.

I wasn't a cheerleader or in the band or choir. I didn't play sports or belong to any clubs. But I could help people.

Number two was Erica Wills. Writing about her now makes me break out in prickly guilt. Mostly I've blocked out the whole Erica experience. She was the girl who needed a bra before the rest of us. The one who was allowed to wear make-up to school first. A truly beautiful girl, model quality. She'd wear the shortest skirts and cleavage revealing tops. She had a fan base of girls in our grade and the grades behind us who would imitate her, copy her style, and remain devoted to her even when she teased them, swore her head off at them, or ridiculed what they said or did. She rarely had a good thing to say about anyone or anything. Still people doted on her. Boys fell all over themselves to date her. Of course "date" was a euphemism. Erica was a slut.

She targeted people to mock. I was on the wrong end of that twice. Once in middle school and once in tenth grade. I actually managed to get a date to Homecoming my sophomore year, but my luck ran out when Erica took advantage of the event to humiliate me.

When I put Erica down on the list as number two, I started to obsess about her. I wasn't actually looking for her when I went to the mall, a few weeks after I sent Shelly Ayers away, but I suppose in the back of my mind I knew she hung out there a lot. The only surprising thing about finding her there was that she wasn't with anyone. No little minions holding her shopping bags. No guys drooling over her caustic attention.

"Hey, Erica," I said as I passed where she stood gazing in the windows of Lord & Taylor's.

"Oh my gosh, Laken, it's you. So nice to see you." Like that wasn't the phoniest thing she ever said.

I stopped, looked at the display she'd been ogling, and elbowed my ratty purse toward my back and out of her line of sight. "Yeah, well, are you shopping for anything special?" I felt so lame to ask.

"Oh, um, hey, I've always meant to apologize for being a little out of line at Homecoming. You forgive me, right? I was a little drunk before I even got there." She laughed and turned her attention back to the window display. "See that purse? I'm only ten dollars short. Do you think you could lend me ten?" She smiled super sweetly. She really was gorgeous, perfect white teeth, still too much make-up, but Hollywood-ready.

Why on earth would I do her a favor? Out of nowhere an idea slammed into my head. "Sure." I wrestled my bag back around and fished out a couple of bills. "Um, Erica, I, uh, I'm having a party tonight. If you want to come, bring your friends. My parents will be gone." What did I think I was doing? Had I changed? Was I suddenly free from hate? Because up until that moment I'd harbored some pretty awful feelings toward Erica and another girl, Melissa, who had both ruined my one and only Homecoming date. But a party … if she came with friends maybe I could gain some acceptance. If she came alone … maybe I could … what? Take her to the lab? Definitely. She needed help, didn't she? She was ruining her life. So promiscuous. I could send her to a time when she'd have to keep her legs crossed to fit in.

"Thanks, Laken, you're a sweetheart." She swiped the bills from my hand and added, "And I'll be sure to tell everyone about your party. It'll be fun, right?"

It wasn't fun. She came all right, with friends. Friends who were angry they had to supply the beer themselves. They made a mess of our house. Erica got wasted and passed out on my bed. Her friends left and after I cleaned things up I considered driving Erica home. But I took her to the time machine instead.

She actually got two trips in the machine that night. It was pretty awful and afterwards I didn't need to google her to see if she had a history in the past— I knew she didn't. I'll write out the sordid details for you later. I don't want to gross you out just yet.

Another girl missing.

2. ~~Erica Wills~~

Our town already had a Bermuda triangle reputation. I blocked the whole Erica thing out of my thoughts and went on to number 3 and then the rest.

3. ~~Ciera Nielson~~
4. ~~Melissa Poznansky~~
5. ~~Cara Branicki~~
6. ~~Megan Hodges~~

I spaced out the disappearances when people got panicky about the apparent epidemic of teen runaways. There was also talk that they'd been snatched away to be sold into the sex slave trade.

Then, late fall, a new girl transferred in. You, Skylar Stone.

You scuffed slowly into my second hour English class that Monday morning and the teacher sat you right behind me. We didn't have the same lunch hour, but we ended up having another class together: fifth hour science. Our science teacher, Mr. Schemanski, moved me out of my group and had me tutor you to help you catch up. I didn't tell you then, but I had a rep among the teachers as dependable and helpful, but they all thought I wasn't working up to my potential. I think my mom told Mr. Schemanski to push me harder. Maybe he thought my working with you was a way to do that.

The thing was I didn't need pushing if I was interested in the subject. My dad taught me about time dilation and relative velocity symmetrics. And my mom bounced her theories off me on metabolic depression in endotherms and how she was working on hyperphagia as it related to time travel. I had my own theories too. I guess the only child of a couple of science nerds was bound to exhibit the same interests.

I stared at you like Schemanski would study a specimen under a microscope. I examined your hair, your face, your clothes, and your shoes and ignored the ripples of déjà vu.

"I'm Laken," I said.

You said, "Cool name." Thanks for that, by the way.

I looked you straight in the eyes and felt like I'd been looking into them the last seventeen years. It really threw me. Remember how I rambled then? I said, "My mom named me after her best friend from high school who was one of countless girls and one boy in our town who, in the last fifty years, just disappeared." That had to sound stupid. You made me nervous for some reason.

"I've heard the rumors." You just ignored my blathering. "So, there was a girl named Laken who disappeared, huh? Do you ever go by just Lake? 'Cause it'd be cool if kids called us Lake and Sky."

So that was how destiny was going to kick me? Suddenly my secret activity didn't seem so charitable any more. It was like I was having a chemical reaction to you, Skylar Stone. I felt guilty. Like I was looking into the eyes of justice. And you, just by making the Lake and Sky comment, had convicted me. It sure

16

seemed like destiny had sent me a friend to put me back on the "straight and narrow."

I changed. A little bit. Right that second. And I changed more each day as I got to know you better.

We became close friends. I had no time anymore to sneak people into the lab and do the disappearing act. We were at each other's house as much as time allowed, whenever I didn't have to be at the lab. At school you were my only real friend, the only one I wanted to talk to. I hadn't tried to climb that slippery ladder called popularity, not since that incident with my first period. But suddenly we were on everyone's radar. Laken and Skylar. Lake and Sky. We went up a couple rungs all at once. But I didn't want to be popular. I didn't want to be noticed.

My mom was overly inquisitive about you. She practically jumped out of her skin when I told her I'd been tutoring a new girl with an unusual name. She got the 'Lake and Sky' thing right away. She was excited I had a good friend, but tried not to show it too much. Maybe she thought her enthusiasm would turn me off the friendship. Actually I thought it was sweet and a little sad, too, because she had lost someone close to her when she was my age. The girl she named me after meant an awful lot to her. Probably like how much you were starting to mean to me. I pretty much loved you, Sky—had an instant connection with you—right from that day we met.

You and I hung out a lot. Five months passed.

I didn't go near the time machine again unless my dad asked me to, to take notes as he "disappeared" a mouse or two.

Chapter 3

I'*ll be there in 10 min,* I texted you. It was spring break, April 2020, and like every other junior we were stuck in the suburbs. Not even the seniors were somewhere warm thanks to some global flu thing. At least it was an early spring and the snow was gone.

I threw my new designer bag on the passenger seat and headed to your house five minutes away. My awesome bag had just about everything in it except money. We were going to Walgreen's and not just to shop for hair dye and make-up. Remember that historic day? We were going to apply for summer jobs and then I'd promised to take you to my parents' lab.

I pulled up and you darted out of the house and yanked open the side door. I remember that you pushed several strands of your recently bleached hair out of your eyes as you looked at my big bag taking up the whole seat.

"Just throw it in the backseat, Sky."

"That's okay, Laken, I'll hold your bag." Yup, you knew better than to throw my costly name brand bag anywhere. You squirmed into the seat and balanced my bag and your equally huge purse on your knees.

"What do you have in here? It's heavy."

I backed out of the driveway and mumbled, "Oh, the usual." What made my bag particularly heavy was the five-pound brick attached to my dad's lab keys.

I glanced over as I took the car out of reverse and watched your face. I knew you'd open the bag and look.

"Are these the keys?"

I couldn't help snorting. "Well, duh."

"So you're really going to take me to the lab? You're sure they're not coming home until tonight?"

"Positive," I said, though I'll tell you now I wasn't absolutely sure. My parents had a habit of disappearing for overnight trips. R and R, they called it. They worked long hours at the lab so they deserved the rest and relaxation. I didn't mind being left alone. They used to give me advanced notice, but then I threw that party for Erica and didn't clean up well enough. Mom and dad stopped telling me when they were going. Sometimes I'd find a note or get a text in the morning saying they'd been 'called away.' But like I said, I didn't mind. It wasn't like they left me alone for more than a day.

"And no one will be at the lab?"

"Nope, not during Thanksgiving, Christmas, or spring break." Or, I thought, three in the morning, my preferred operating time last fall. I'd brought all the girls on my list here in the middle of the night. It was going to be different doing this in the daytime.

"I can't believe we're going to break in."

I flicked my turn indicator on and headed toward the drug store. "It's not breaking and entering if I have the keys. And my parents own the place. You're okay with this, right?"

"Sure. All that stuff your mom told me about the bear hibernation research was really fascinating. And since I want to be a veterinarian, well, you understand."

I did understand. You were such a fanatic about animals—are you still?—and the lab had some animals, well, mostly mice, but that was going to be your focus, not mine. I had an ulterior motive for taking you to the lab. I needed you to help me undo something awful. If it was even possible. I was certain I'd be able to convince you, Sky, once you saw the lab. In fact, I was positive. I'd already dropped a ton of hints in order to massage your conscience into acceptance. Goodness knows I'd been massaging my own conscience ever since I'd started "helping" others.

But first the normal stuff: apply for jobs at the store.

"Why do you suppose he has the keys attached to a brick?" you asked, flipping through the radio stations until you settled on the latest song by Blue Nine Sistas.

I shrugged my shoulders.

"Are you sure the keys will work? Have you been to the lab recently? Have they hired an intern yet? Will he be there?"

Skylar, why did you always do that? Ask so many questions without waiting for the answers, I mean. I had to think fast and spit back the answers, "Yes, they haven't changed the locks. I was there yesterday. No intern yet and he wouldn't work Saturdays anyway. Okay?"

I pulled into the parking lot and before we got out of the car where anyone could hear us, I reminded you that I'd practically grown up at the lab. I'd go there every day after school, though not quite as much since you arrived. What I didn't tell you yet, what I was afraid to tell you, was that before you moved here I'd helped abused girls flee their dysfunctional lives. The lab was essential to helping those poor victims. Especially if they didn't want help. I sure hoped you'd understand.

I was super nervous to unload it on you, but sometimes everything must be risked for the sake of, well, everything. And after what I'd learned about the sister of one of my victims, I didn't think I had a choice.

We hurried into the store as the weather changed and it started to drizzle that cold April rain. On days like that I wished my parents had invented a place machine instead of a time machine.

We were distracted first by the jewelry counter. You looked for earrings and necklaces. My eye was drawn to an odd charm that hung from a plain silver chain.

"Unbelievable. Skylar, look at this." I pulled the chain off the display rack and set the charm on the glass counter.

The clerk, looking beyond bored, watched me run my finger over the design. She offered an explanation, "That's blown glass. The lake is floating in a background that represents the sky or the galaxy. Or the universe, whatever. It's $42."

"We should each get one. Do you have another?"

"No, sorry. Just one."

My heart sank. It was a beautiful pendant and I wanted it. It seemed like the perfect emblem of our friendship: lake and sky. And maybe I was looking for something to cement our bond before I put a strain on it.

"I'll pay half and we can share it," you whispered. You were—I mean, are—the most awesome friend ever.

"Deal." Of course that took most of the money I had with me—the last of my Christmas money. Though I had access to that treasure chest, I never took any money other than for time travels.

The music that was piped through the ceiling changed then, as if someone were flipping through the radio stations until they settled on the latest song by Blue Nine Sistas. It gave me chills since the lyrics kept commanding *don't do it, don't do it.*

21

But we did it. We bought the pendant and you—best friend that you were and are—insisted that I wear it first. You bought a couple other items, personal stuff, and we picked up a couple of their job application forms. Then we waited out the storm by reading all of the humorous greeting cards. Remember the one about the buns? So funny. We finally left when there was a break in the clouds.

You were all hyped about the hourly wages. You did the math on what we'd make working ten, fifteen, or twenty hours a week until school let out. It was only simple arithmetic but you did it so fast that I was impressed. I knew right then that I'd made the right decision to ask you to accompany me back to 1994, where I'd mistakenly sent Megan Hodges.

There'd been a lot of media coverage after Megan's disappearance last fall. She was number six, my best good deed, or so I thought. When I picked her up she was sporting bruises on her arms and face. After she was reported missing the police never interviewed me. As far as anyone knew we'd never met, never had any classes together, never gone to the same parties. I sure wasn't about to sound like a psycho and claim I'd sent her into the past with a time machine. Anyway, her disappearance coincided with the discovery of a badly decomposed body not too far from the lab. That news sent a blast of both guilt and regret straight to my heart, not to mention fear. I was more than a little worried that the police might want to see what was in the lab.

I guess I was zoned out thinking about that when your voice broke through my thoughts, "Laken, turn off the wipers. The squeaking and scraping is annoying."

The sun peeked out for a couple minutes, but more clouds rolled in as we turned onto the long driveway leading to Mitchell Labs. Ominous, I thought, and as creepy as the song on the radio: *... waiting for you, hating for you, diggin' a grave that's baiting for you ...*

"Won't there be security?" you asked.

"Well, there is and there isn't," I said. "My parents bought an old monastery that sits on twenty secluded acres. They totally remodeled the inside, but left the outside looking pretty run-down."

We took the last curve and you gasped as you saw the crumbling stone facade and the broken windows. Perfect reaction. I braked too hard and sent wet gravel spraying. It sounded like how the Blue Nine Sistas end their songs with hissing.

I finished the explanation, "Those are boarded up on the inside with concrete block walls on the other side. So, even if somebody broke the rest of the window out and took a hatchet to those boards they still couldn't get in. That's the security."

"Oh," was all you said. You sat forward, straining the seat belt and wrinkling your forehead into a question. You looked so concerned and hesitant that I resolved to tell you everything. Or almost everything.

You stared at the columns and arches, the small tower windows, and the gratings that made the front look like a medieval place of dungeons and torture. It made an even more intimidating impression in the middle of the night when my headlights would sweep across the stones and promise ghosts. It took some extra persuasion then to get my pet projects, the abused girls, to leave the car. You wouldn't be that reluctant; you trusted me. And it was still daylight.

I drove the car around to the back where there was a twelve-foot-high gate topped with razor wire.

"Brick, please."

You dug into my bag and silently handed me what my dad called the 'lab slab' or the 'block lock' or just the 'frickin' brick' when he was in a hurry. You wouldn't expect that something so heavy could get misplaced, but it happened a lot. What foresight he had to make so many. It was cumbersome to hold it out the window and finagle the right key into the gate lock, but I'd done it before. The gate swung forward and we drove in and down an incline.

"Wait a second," I said. I turned the car off, stuck the car key under the mat, and got out. I went back to jam a stick in the iron gate to keep it from closing and locking. I only just thought of that. If we came back from the past and couldn't get to the car we'd be found out. And I sure wasn't going to take that heavy brick with us. My bag was going to be stuffed as it was. I glanced up at the sharp wire and remembered your question about security. I couldn't help letting the corners of my mouth turn up.

You got out of the car carrying both our bags on one shoulder with the brick and keys in your left hand.

"That way." I pointed toward a path of wood chips that showed no footprints. We reached the massive back door together and I used both the gate key and the second key to gain our entrance. The door opened without a sound as those somber clouds let loose with a penetrating rain again.

There were two more keys on the brick; I'd need to use both later and then hide the brick somewhere outside. You would have to let me back in. I hoped it would stop raining by then.

I flicked on the lights before the door closed, revealing a long passageway and another locked door. I used the third key, my dad's idea of adequate security.

Once we were in the main area I could tell that you were impressed, Sky. The fluorescent lights gave it that familiar high school classroom feel that we were used to, right? But the smell was a cross between the dentist's office and a furniture store. With a hint of wet dog.

When you handed me my bag you said, "I didn't expect it to be so modern after seeing that run-down exterior. And I'd never suspect that it'd be so bright and open. I thought there'd be different rooms for offices, research, animal studies—" Your voice trailed off as you spotted the row of cages along the far wall next to a mammoth arched door.

"Go ahead. You can play with the mice. They won't bite." I walked behind you through the maze of tables and desks. You'd think fifty people worked here instead of only my parents and occasionally an intern or two. You were right about there being other rooms though. The old monastery bedrooms were monks' cells that now housed all kinds of things from computers to supplies to living, breathing experiments. And the topmost room, the one with four boarded up windows, hid the mother of ultimate inventions: the time machine. All four keys on the brick were needed for entrance.

I watched you study the cages. There were maybe fifty mice all with plenty of food and water. Somebody, not me, had cleaned the cages recently. That was odd.

I pulled out a chair and sat at the last desk by the cages. "Aren't they cute? I used to train them."

"To do what?"

25

"Walk backwards, stand up, spin. Stuff like that." I didn't mention I got my heart broken more than once when my pets died or disappeared. I adjusted the clasp of the glass-blown pendant, pulling it to the back of my neck. I was so happy that you insisted I wear it first.

I remember your hand hovering over the cage door. "What do the colored markings mean?"

"It's dye. When we get a new batch we give them a new color, a birthday tattoo. The orange ones have been here the longest, then the yellow, green, and so on. Like the rainbow."

"No reds?" You scanned the cages.

I shook my head. The reds were sleeping deeper than death in one of the monk's rooms, safe in a bed of cedar shavings, waiting to awaken and submit to mom's research into their metabolism, energy, tissue and organ degeneration, and any aftereffects of sleeping longer than they would have lived. My parents never made anything off limits to my curiosity—not since I turned twelve—and I had free rein to read their hand-written notes and click through their computer graphs of data. In fact, I never told you that I was part of the research. I'm not kidding. My mom drew a minuscule bit of blood from me periodically for part of her data. A lot of her findings were pretty technical, but when I got the idea to help troubled girls escape the beatings and horrible home situations, I paid a lot more attention to the science of those experiments. I have a pretty high IQ, not that I'm bragging, yours is higher, for sure.

Science connected us all. Me, you, my parents, the missing teens. It was providential how a week before my having you over to study for a science test inspired me to double check—Google again—my last two victims. What I discovered with a simple name search pushed me to this edge and to include you on my first time travel.

Chapter 4

You stepped back from the mice cages holding one whose white fur had a splotch of blue dye across the back. "We're twins," you said, holding him up near your ear. Yeah, that blue streak in your hair was pretty awesome.

I smiled. "I think there's more resemblance in the nose and whiskers." I was just teasing I hope you know.

"Poor thing," you cooed, caressing the creature. "Don't be afraid. They're not going to hurt you. The experiments won't harm you. You'll just sleep. Sleep." You kept repeating the word like the mouse had already been given the sleep agent and needed a lullaby to finish the job. I barely heard you whisper, "I wish I could set you free outside."

"Sky, did my mom tell you about all the hibernation experiments?" Two days ago you had come over for dinner and right after we ate my dad asked me to help him move some things in the garage. I suspected that was a ploy so you and mom could plan a surprise party for my upcoming birthday, but when I came back in you were deep in conversation about dosing, injections, and pills versus food additives. That's when I got the idea to time-travel with you.

"What do you mean?"

"You know what I mean. Did she explain the pills?"

"Isn't that like top secret stuff?" You turned to put the mouse back. You were avoiding answering, but honestly Sky, did you think I wouldn't notice how you were sidestepping a straight answer? I so totally get you, you know. That silly question confirmed that you knew about the pills. "Why would she tell me that? We were just talking about hyper-something, you know, how bears eat a ton of stuff before their long winter's sleep."

"Hyperphagia."

"Yeah." You turned to face me but started rummaging through your bag so you didn't have to look at me. I felt an immense urge to spill everything, but I didn't want to freak you out. You thought we were there so I could show you lab rats and a monkey or two, but I needed you there for something epic. I was sure my mom had told you the formula for sleeping through time. That would make things so much easier.

Life was full of coincidences, my dad always said. My mom would shake her head and say there were no coincidences. I almost said so right then. Instead I stood up, lifted the brick with the keys, and told you to follow me. It was time to show you the sleepers.

Reese's cell was the first door on the left. There was a two foot deep alcove slightly wider than the doorway which we squeezed into to see through the glass window my dad had installed. Reese was somewhere around twenty years old when my parents bought her several years ago. She'd spent most of her time here asleep on a cot. As Rhesus monkeys go she was absolutely normal. I didn't get a chance to befriend her before she was tucked in a hooded space blanket and sent off to dreamland, if monkeys dream. Silver electrodes fed data to a computer whose monitor was easily read even through the pint-sized window in the door.

I expected you to be shocked and maybe get weepy, but you stared through the window and acted totally fine with the experiment.

"How long has it been asleep?" you asked.

"It's a she. And she's been out almost four years."

"Holy crap. And there's no feeding tube?"

"No. No food, no water for four years."

Your silence was unreadable. I knew what would go through my head if I were you: I'd wonder if Reese would be normal or brain damaged when she woke up.

Apparently your thoughts took a different direction though. "You'd think its hair, her hair, would all fall out. Wow. Just imagine. Trillions of cells all in stasis. Your mom is a genius."

"I'm glad you think so. The most important thing though is no brain damage." I needed to stress that so there'd be no hesitation when we got to the third floor. "Look over here." I moved a couple feet up the narrow hallway to the next alcove. "This is Mack, a former circus chimp turned science experiment."

His cell was the same eight-by-ten bedroom that some long ago monk slept in and endured a religious routine free of distractions, comfort, and companionship. Mack, however, enjoyed an assortment of distractions: colorful toys, stuffed animals, and even his own computer.

Your shoulder bumped mine as you exclaimed, "He's awake."

No doubt Mack had heard us long before we came down this hallway. He sat calmly on his cot, watching, waiting. Sometimes he could creep me out because he was so well-trained, so human-like.

"He slept for three years and woke up last summer. He remembered all of his training, sign-language, behaviors, etc."

"So no brain damage. That's awesome." You eyed the doorknob. I knew what you were thinking.

"Um, we don't open the door. It's not locked, but Mack is in charge of when he comes out." I lowered my voice, "He's been a little upset since he found himself suddenly outside last week." I sensed a tingle in my armpits, that first niggle of adrenalin seeping out, because I was close to revealing some pretty amazing secrets.

You peeled your attention away from Mack to look at me. Then you glanced at the lock block in my right hand. With all the locks and 'security' I'm sure you wondered how he managed to get out. Time to let the cat out of the bag. "I actually haven't seen Mack in six months. My dad sent him, uh, forward. That is—" I was not telling this right. "—last fall after they were sure the long sleep did no harm to him they took him upstairs." I drew in a quick breath. "There's a time machine. My folks have been working on it virtually since they started dating. It's on the third floor."

I held my breath. Your eyes held an understanding and acceptance that I hadn't expected, so I hurried on. "The time machine is aimed at a grassy mound beyond the monastery gardens. That's farther back. There used to be gardens and paths, meditation areas, you know, and they decided that was the best place to land." My laugh probably sounded nervous and like a lunatic, but that was because I suddenly realized that the time machine was, as I had wished, also a place machine. Your face didn't scrunch into a doubtful wrinkle, but your eyes widened a smidgen, and you stared past me. "Sky? You believe me?"

"Of course." But you didn't blink. "Of course I believe you. This is awesome. Who else knows?" Your gaze returned to my face.

"Oh, I've never told anyone about this." Well, that wasn't exactly true. "You have to promise not to tell a soul. Promise?"

Suddenly I was at your mercy. My parents would kill me for sure; they'd been adamant that I never speak to outsiders about what goes on in the lab and to never, ever talk about time travel. Of course, I'd skirted that fact a half dozen times when I'd used the machine on those other girls. A sliver of adrenaline pierced my heart as I realized all the power in my telling you, Skylar.

Then Mack slammed himself against the door. We both jumped back and I dropped the brick. The knob twisted and Mack let the door swing open. He stood there sniffing the air. And staring at you.

You murmured your promise to keep our secret and then held your hand out to Mack. "I get it." You spoke really softly. "I get it, Mack. Come here. I'm your friend." Mack's eyes were riveted on yours and he continued to sniff. Then suddenly his jaw dropped and it looked like he was smiling. You immediately crouched down and continued to sweet-talk him. "It's okay, Mack. I won't hurt you. Don't be afraid."

I could feel the hairs on my neck bristle. Mack gave a 'ho-ha' panting noise and jumped back into his cell. He slammed the door.

"Huh," I said, picking up the keys, "I thought for a second he liked you. That was a big smile he gave you."

You rose up and shook your head. "That was his fear face, not a smile."

"And you know that because…?"

Gotta love your eye rolls. "Uh, maybe I thought I wanted to be a veterinarian? Maybe I've been to the zoo a hundred times? Maybe I did a project on chimps in captivity? Pick one."

"Okay, but why the fear? You're not a threat."

"Animals sense things. You just told me about the time machine and a shudder went through me like nothing I've ever felt before. Maybe he reacted to that."

I thought about that and started moving us up the hallway toward the stairs. We passed six other cells, most of them empty.

"You kept saying 'I get it.' What did you mean?"

A pale smile crept unto your face before you spoke, "You said Mack was fine after the long sleep and then he, uh, 'time-traveled' and ended up out back. So I get it. I get why your mom is working on hibernation. The time machine doesn't go with the traveler, right? So there'd be no way to get back unless there was another time machine on the other end. If you went to, say, the year 2000 you'd have to live through the years again until you got back to now. But then you'd be older. But if you went back and then ate enough to hibernate through the years, you'd wake up like Reese and Mack and not have aged. Not much anyway."

You did get it. You got it too fast and too well. Coincidence? A muffled ring tone interrupted us and you dug through your bag for your phone. You read the text, smiled, and texted back.

"I have a date. A blind date with a college guy my sister set me up with. Next Saturday."

"Really, Sky? Really? You're going to go out with a college guy? Why would he want to date a high school girl? Do we want to hang out with middle-schoolers? Think about it. He's probably some ugly loser."

You tapped your phone and held it out. The picture was quite clear. "Oh." The guy was mad hot, that face would definitely make me want to change my time-travel plans.

Okay, I could deal with your dating a college guy. Maybe he'd have a friend for me. But at that moment I wanted to

33

concentrate on my problem and even though you were smart and caught on faster than I expected I only had a few hours before my parents would be back. Timing was everything.

You dropped your phone into your bag and I unlocked the door to the tower. We climbed to the second floor. It was an open area, but crammed with supplies. "Open your purse again. We're taking a load of these high protein, high calorie bars. Oh, and they're high fat, too."

"Laken."

Our eyes met. The look you gave me was like when my mom caught me stealing cookies. I swallowed hard.

"Don't you want to ask me if I'll time-travel with you first?" Your stern look melted. "You don't have to convince me, Lake. I'm in. In fact, well, it was your mom who convinced me to go with you."

I might have gasped then. "She doesn't know I'm planning this. Nobody could know."

"Well, maybe she only suspects, then. But, she sure made it seem like the world balanced on me knowing how her hibernation pills work."

No, no, uh-uh. No way do they know what I've already done. Unless … could it be that I've already time-traveled? Maybe some future-me came back and told them. No, that didn't make sense … not then it didn't … but now, well, that's why I'm writing this down for you.

You touched my arm. "Laken. Forget it. Maybe I was reading too much into the lecture she gave me. Come on, what's next?"

I couldn't afford to get distracted by what my mom may or may not have deduced. I refocused. What was next was to tell you about Megan. Without realizing it I had filled my bag with twice as many of the survival bars, because once we got to 1994 I'd also need some for Megan Hodges—if she was still alive and we could find her. We absolutely *had* to find her though. Her parents were not going to give up looking and eventually the well-hidden trail would lead to me, the lab, my parents and the time machine. The consequences of that could mean a life on the run or a life in prison.

And who knows what horrible future the world would have if the government got its hands on the machine.

Chapter 5

I shook those terrible thoughts out of my head and got back to filling my bag. We'd need lots of water too, but I counted on finding plenty where we were going, but just in case I grabbed two LifeStraws out of the survival box. We'd be able to drink from a mud puddle with them if we had to. I also pulled out three Mylar thermal blankets. We'd need them for the steady insulated warmth they'd provide when we had to hibernate.

"Why three?" you asked.

I glanced at the clock on the stone wall. Two fifteen. There was plenty of time to tell you about Megan. I told you to sit on the stool I used to do inventory. I perched myself on that metal trunk that was filled with old currency and silver coins. This was going to be a life-changing confession; I'd been lying awake at night trying to figure out how to fix things.

"Do you remember when you first moved here and there was a lot of publicity about a girl named Megan who'd gone missing?"

You nodded too slowly.

I bit my lip and went on, "I did it."

No scream, no protest, no 'you're kidding!' You froze mid nod and then resumed the head bobbing but with the tiniest of smiles playing on your face, like you were ready to believe whatever your best friend told you. Thanks for that.

"I sent her to 1994." I drummed my fingers on the money-filled trunk and waited for your reaction.

"Did you go with her?"

I was surprised by your question. Did my face show it? Such instant belief was too good to be true. "No, I didn't go with her. But I need to go now. I have to find her and bring her back. I was wrong to send her in the first place. She wasn't like the others."

"There were others?" That's when your face changed. There was the briefest moment when my best friend wasn't my best friend, but I was confident that as soon as I started to speak, you'd believe me.

"They were abused. Beat up. From terrible dysfunctional families. The first one, Shelly Ayers, was somebody I knew from middle school. I ran into her right after I got my license. Well, not physically. I saw her walking, or rather limping, along the bus route. I stopped to give her a ride. She was a mess. To make a long story short, I brought her here, asked my parents if she could sleep on a cot, live here, and help out with the animals in exchange for food. They didn't like the idea. It was so not like them. I mean, they wouldn't even consider it. But they did say Shelly could stay at our house that night."

"So you snuck back here with her?"

"Yeah. Three in the morning. Spooky as a graveyard. We'd been talking all night and we both knew she couldn't go home again. You can't imagine what she'd already been through. I asked her what if she could live any time she wanted to—when would that be?"

"And she said 1994."

"No, not Shelly. She picked 1963. She had a thing for the Beatles. She liked the idea of the 60s. Free love. Hippies. Drugs. We had just studied that era. Anyway, I took her up to the third floor and told her to lie down in the machine and I'd magically send her to 1963. She probably thought it was a game. I gave her five hundred dollars in old bills from, uh, this trunk I'm sitting on, and told her to never say she was from the future or she'd be sent to a mental hospital. Then I set the machine and waved at her. She waved back, crossed her arms over her heart, and closed her eyes like she was playing along. I closed my eyes, too, and said a little prayer. When I looked a few seconds later she'd disappeared like a shadow, like a dream."

"Do you think she made it?"

"I know she did. I googled her. She kept her name, made a fortune then set up a foundation for abused kids. She died a few years ago. Before I sent her back."

"Weird. And you're sure it was her?"

"Positive. I've googled the others, too, but they must have changed their names."

"Or didn't make it."

"I don't like to think that." I jumped off the trunk and started pacing along the racks of old clothes and costumes. I really didn't want to think about that—because of Erica. "Anyway, Megan Hodges, the last one I made to disappear, just before you moved here, went to 1994, mostly because that was where Cara, who was number five, went. I didn't change the settings." You nodded like you were keeping up with my story. "I didn't get a chance to ask Megan where she'd prefer to go. I'd been to a party at the park—I was sort of in disguise, just checking it out— and I saw her; she was stoned out of her head. Someone said she'd fallen earlier, tripped over her own fluorescent green shoes, they said, and I could see a big bruise on her cheek. I walked her to the restrooms and asked her questions."

"About abuse? About her family?"

"Yeah, and she gave me some weird answers. She said her parents put her sister in the hospital and she was next. I guided her to my car and brought her to the lab. I didn't have the keys of course, but there was an intern working here late, well actually he was babysitting Mack who had just awakened the week before. He let us in. It was warm in the lab and Megan started pulling off her windbreaker over her head. I could see more purpling on her ribs and her arms were covered in bruises. John, the intern, was understanding about letting her sleep in one of the cells and promised not to tell my folks. In fact he helped me get her there because she was suddenly dizzy. After he went back to the main room I managed to walk her up two flights of stairs. And then—" I snapped my fingers. "Poof. I sent her to '94 and went home. John never said anything to the police. I don't think he knew she was the missing girl. She didn't look anything that night like the pictures of her they put on the TV. She'd been made up like a rock star." I plunked myself back down on the trunk, out of breath but wonderfully unburdened. You said nothing.

I thought I could hear somebody moving around downstairs. Mack, of course. He could roam up and down the hall if he wanted to, but I locked the other doors behind us so the lab and the tower were off limits to him. He could make a mess of things if he got into the wrong areas. My dad tested him and jokingly said that time travel had made Mack smarter and calmer. I wanted to believe that because I was getting more nervous about taking this trip.

"So …" I drew out the syllable and waited for some kind of response from you.

"I believe you, Lake, but, uh, what's the rest of the story? About Megan? Why do you have to retrieve her? It seems to me that anybody could go to the past and make a fortune. She might not want to come back."

"Well, the other girls were believed to be runaways. Nobody filed a missing person's report on them. That's how little their parents cared about them. They were probably afraid the police would find out about the abuse." (Well, that was my theory then, but now, after all that's happened, you'll probably agree that maybe, just maybe, those girls were in two places at once, kind of like you.)

I took a big breath and continued, "But Megan's parents made a big deal about her disappearance. I avoided watching the news and walked away whenever anyone talked about her. I purposely tried not to know anything about it. Like I said, I googled her right after and there was nothing. Not one thing." I paused and cracked a couple knuckles. "I thought she must have changed her name. I tried again last week. There was still nothing about her, but there was an obituary for her sister. She died. Those bruises, they weren't from beatings, they were from a disease. Her sister had leukemia. I think Megan did, too. I mean does."

Your frown mimicked my own. You barely whispered, "But she could be dead by now, too."

"Not if we go back to exactly the same time. It'll work. I know it will."

"Or," your face had a light bulb glow, "we could go back to the day before and catch her as she arrives." You gave a scary laugh. "Wouldn't that freak her out? Or, hey, she might not even believe that she time-traveled. We could just give her food, the pills, and voila."

I laughed along with you. Wow, you were quick with ideas. I shouldn't have been surprised. I helped you catch up in science class last fall, but since then you got higher grades on every test. Sorry if I seemed rude to dismiss your idea, but I remembered the exact time settings and I didn't want to take a single chance of screwing this up. If it worked, I wanted to repeat the process and go back and get all of my "clients" because … well, I might not be perfect, but I really wasn't a serial killer. The body the police discovered maybe didn't have anything to do with me, maybe it wasn't Cara or Megan or Ciera … but maybe it was. And maybe I, we, could change things.

"So you'll go with me for sure?" Your slow nod was answer enough. I wasn't sure you'd come, but I never should have doubted it. It was destiny, undeniably—though I was still betting on being able to change certain destinies. I got off the trunk, opened it, and handed you fifty dollars and stuffed another two twenties in my jeans. Ninety bucks could go twice as far in '94. "Don't get this mixed up with any money minted in this century."

"I won't. These do look different."

"Uh huh. I think our clothes are okay though. We don't need to change. Come on. Let's go up."

I took the sixteen steps to the third floor two at a time, my excitement scarcely under control. I couldn't believe you had accepted everything I told you without blinking. I was ecstatic. I unlocked all four tumblers and pushed the steel door wide. There were six windows in the top of the tower, but they were all boarded over except two. It was raining harder, but the sky wasn't so dark that sufficient light couldn't illuminate the round room. You got a good look at the ghostly gray machine. It could have come out of a horror movie. Then I switched on the lights and the reflections off the metal parts and the stark white top and sides gave it a distinctly hospital vibe. That could still be pretty scary. I stood next to the control panel, a vast array of levers, switches, and screens for readouts of coordinates, dates, pressure numbers and other data. You stepped forward and pushed a lungful of air between your lips, not quite producing a whistle. I didn't know what you expected, but you had to be impressed.

"Your parents built this?" Your jaw trembled. "I can't believe it."

"What does it look like to you?"

"Like, like an MRI machine and a microwave got together and had a baby. A big baby." You took a tentative step forward clutching your bag to your chest as if for protection.

"Don't touch anything." I set my bag down and brushed my left hand over the controls. Since Mack's forward time travel there hadn't been any other experiments. I didn't know why my dad didn't do shorter trips in the meantime, while he watched for aftereffects. Of course, Mack's trip was short compared to my sending girls to '63, '94, and also the '70s and '80s. I turned the machine on and expected to see a readout of March 26, 2020, but everything had apparently defaulted to today's date, April 4. Strange. I changed the setting to Wednesday, June 15, 1994. There was no calibration for exact time, but I did need to input longitude and latitude. My mother insisted that the gentle hill behind the labyrinth of gardens was the safest spot to 'land' on a time travel. Nothing had ever been built there so there was little risk you'd end up melded inside a chimney or a wall, though I worried about tree trunks. I knew the coordinates by heart though my dad had fumed last year about the government changing the global positioning system whenever there was a homeland security threat. No point could ever be regarded as solid or fixed, he said, but had to be calculated in relation to the southern cable satellite, which was more reliable. I stared at my entry then made a slight adjustment.

"Okay, it's set. Now for the hard part."

You visibly gulped. "We get in the machine?" You were still staring at the platform which, though as large as a bed, did not invite you to nestle in for a cozy nap.

"No. We need to prop open all the doors so I can take the brick of keys out beyond the gate and hide it. Otherwise we won't have a way back in when we return."

"You know what, Laken? We should just plan on returning right now. Maybe that's the noise we heard downstairs. We're already back and we followed ourselves in. And we're staying out of sight because ... because it'd probably make some time paradox if we see ourselves."

I nodded at you, but I wasn't agreeing. I'd had that discussion with my dad numerous times. I knew all about Novikov's self-consistency theory, the theory of multiple universes, the erased timeline hypothesis and more, but this wasn't the time to summarize for you that a paradox could be something that happens despite being contradictory or seemingly impossible. You seemed to think a paradox had to be fatal and I didn't want to think about that right then. "Well, maybe, but to be on the safe side I want to hide the keys outside."

We had plenty of things in our bags to use to prop open the third floor door, the stairwell door, and the door into the lab. My biggest fear was that Mack would come out and undo everything so as we passed his cell I checked that he was inside and locked him in. With any luck we'd be back in what would seem like only a few hours to him, or maybe, like you said, we were already back, waiting for the brick.

Anyway, you stayed at the main door of the lab and watched me run through the rain and out the gate. I was super careful to wedge that stick between the bars even though taking my time was making me get soaked to the skin. I went toward the gardens and stopped at the crumbling wishing well. I placed the brick inside the once decorative well with the key side down. I didn't give it a second look, but I did take one very wet moment to stare at the old pump house that was covered in vines. That was the safe place that I heard my parents discuss once. They'd never opened the door, or so my dad had told me. It wasn't locked, just jammed stuck. It wouldn't budge. I know, I tried. There was also one dark window that I'd always tried to see through growing up. I'd seen my dad peering in, but he wouldn't lift me up to let me look in. So when he wasn't around I used to jump as high as I could to try to peek in, but I never got close. I hadn't done that in years.

Rain dribbled down my neck. The temptation to look in now that I was tall enough was blocked by the thought of what I would, or wouldn't see.

I hurried back. Once through the gate I tossed the stick aside and let the lock latch. The rain stopped but there was no sun yet to shine its approval on our plan. I slipped on the wood chips and you yelped out a 'be careful' in the same tone my mother would use.

Step one: convince you to go with me. Check.

Step two: collect supplies. Check.

Step three: hide keys for return. Check.

Step four: Make sure we haven't forgotten anything.

Chapter 6

I grinned like an idiot and hopped from foot to foot in my impatience to get going. Then I did a few mental forehead slaps as we snaked around all the research desks on the main floor, me leaving a wet trail. I'd forgotten the most important thing: the sleep agents. Before John up and quit last Christmas he'd been working on filling varying sized capsules with the exact dosages of sleep agent my mom invented. We didn't have an intern this semester so I'd been watching my mom do it, but she never let me help other than to count out ten capsules to a case and mark the case with the capsule size. The SU07 had 28 milliliters of volume, that was the largest and mom put a super concentrated batch in those. There were trays of the different capsule sizes and I had to be extra careful to keep the 10s separate from the hardly smaller 11s, which held 10 ml. That could be confusing. The tiniest ones only held .2 ml. I asked her why all the different sizes and amounts and how she knew how many milligrams would fill a milliliter. She eagerly spit out a hibernation formula that lost me in two seconds flat. I hoped to heck it wouldn't be hard for you, Sky, to figure it out.

I pulled you toward the inside front wall instead of going toward the door we'd propped open by the mice cages.

You whined at me, "Hey, you're getting me wet."

"Sorry, but I almost forgot, we don't want to go into the past without the pills to get us back here." I opened a file cabinet and started taking out various cases. "These will put us in a kind of suspended animation for years. We'll hibernate like bears, bundled in our space blankets and nourished by all the food we'll gorge ourselves on."

You remarked that the labels were strange and I explained how the capsule numbers didn't correspond like you'd think. "My mom told me why. All I remember is the largest one is different. One of those pills is worth ten years of sleep. The rest are less potent; the .2 milliliter pill puts you out for twenty-four hours."

"Does it matter how much we weigh?"

I lifted my head and pushed back a few wet strands of hair and stared at you. "Good question. Reese is a lot smaller than Mack and she got the same amount. Mack's been awake for months."

"All right, I've got a confession. Your mom did tell me about the pills. I thought she meant a trip to outer space when she said a traveler could sleep for a specific length of time. She said to add a zero and divide by two for each day. I think I understand that." You tapped the top of the 24 ml box and said, "A size twenty-four pill would equal a hundred and twenty days. The eighteens would put you out for ninety days. That's three months. It's pretty easy. But she also said that men, or women over a hundred fifty pounds, would have to calculate with a divisor of two point two."

"Are you sure?"

"Yeah, but we're both under one fifty so we can divide by two. Easy. What about Megan? How much does she weigh?"

"I have no idea." I looked at the assorted cases of pills and tried to remember what it felt like to help Megan up to the tower. "Yeah, she seemed to be about our size. Well, we need six of the big pills for sure." I started to shiver. The cold rain had gotten to me and the pressure of this whole big thing was mounting.

Suddenly I couldn't do the math to figure out exactly how many pills to take, so I dumped ten or fifteen of each size into my bag. There was a little spray bottle marked Hiber-wake and I started to grab that too. But since it was the only one, it would be sure to be missed.

"That should do it," you agreed.

I hoped so, now what else was I forgetting? Was this a stupid, lame brain idea? We could disappear into the past and be two more missing persons for this town to obsess about. I was two seconds away from calling the whole thing off. Then my mind flashed on the obituary of Megan's sister. Her parents were devastated. Wouldn't it be awesome if we could return one of their daughters to them? I shivered again, but in a good way.

We headed toward the door just as we heard a noise in the hall.

You lifted your eyebrows. "Mack?"

I wasn't so sure. Now I wished I had checked the pump house.

"Must be Mack," I said. I picked up the space blanket we'd used to wedge the door open and let you pass through first. I tested the door to make sure it closed and latched. I wriggled against a tingle of dread that this whole plan could collapse quite easily if the next door wedge hadn't held and we were trapped in this wing of the old building. I slung my bag over my shoulder, looking neither right or left at the alcoved doorways, and raced to the other end of the hall. Your bag was nearly bent in half by the heavy stairway door, but it had held.

"You're leaving a mess," you said as you came up behind me, not in any hurry at all.

I looked at the few damp spots, a smudge or two of mud, and ignored your concern. No big deal. I could quickly change my jeans and top, but there was nothing I could do about my shoes or hair. If I was lucky they'd be dry by 1994. I laughed to myself.

In the supply room I left my wet jeans on the floor and found another pair in the '90s section that fit me. Ripped knees, faded denim. I pulled on a plain white t-shirt and picked a plaid long-sleeved shirt to go over it. You held out a silver mini-skirt and asked me if I wouldn't rather time-travel in style. I gave you a little assassinating smile. You returned an intense eye roll and hung the skirt back up.

"Okay, I'm ready." I picked up my wet things and threw them over the chair. If everything turned out as I planned I'd be changing back into those things soon.

I grabbed a bottle of water off the shelf and chugged half of it down. Then I put three more full ones in my bag. You did the same. Had we really thought of everything?

I was completely out of breath and it wasn't from taking the steps to the third floor two at a time again. It was nerves. Fear. Excitement. Apprehension.

The swivel chair still held its place keeping the steel door from closing. A stream of sunlight raced across the floor from one of the windows. If only I'd waited five minutes I could have hidden the brick after that rain shower and not have had to change clothes.

"Um," you pivoted from one foot to the other, "there's not a bathroom up here, is there?"

I shook my head and realized I'd been holding back the same urge. "We'd have to set up all the doors again. The bathroom is in the main lab."

"It's okay. I can hold it. Probably just nervous excitement." You sucked in your cheeks and crossed your legs. That made me smile. Sometimes, Sky, you're such a comedian.

"Lie down on your back inside the machine and hold your bag on your stomach." I guess because I gave them so nonchalantly my instructions sounded funny. But this wasn't funny, this was the scariest, most serious part. My trusting best friend—you—obeyed with a chortle, and I laughed, too, a sort of snot snicker.

I set my bag down next to you like I was saving my spot, eyed the edges of the metal, and mentally measured the distance I'd have to run and jump. Although I'd sent a half dozen others into the past, I'd never actually been in the time machine myself. I knew I only had four seconds from the time I hit the switch. I needed to run, leap, land, and make sure all extremities were inside with you or when you got to 1994 you might have arrived with a puddle instead of a Lake. Would you have laughed if I'd said that out loud?

Chapter 7

Time Machine Date: 1994

Everybody knows some hours can seem like a year. My sixth hour class felt like that. You could practically hear kids' eyes glazing over. I guess I expected my first time trip to be just as drawn-out, but I was wrong. In time travel, years only lasted seconds.

I had vague perceptions of space movement, of rolling downward, and of a horrible dream in which my strength failed and tremendous evil was just out of sight. All of that was so dark and so indistinct in my mind that I was sure it belonged to another life, not mine, and yet it mixed with mine in a perfectly acceptable balance of fantasy and science. I never understood how a cell phone worked or how you could hear someone on the other side of the world in an instant. Or how movies and pictures could be sent through the air and ended up on my computer, TV, or phone. I'll probably never understand how my parents built a time machine, but I used it as easily as sending a text.

I was hunched over my bag, exactly like when I landed on it after my panicked leap into the machine an instant before. I fully expected to suffer a fall and not be stationary, but my experience was virtually motionless. The lake and sky pendant dangled from my neck, finishing the swing it started in 2020. My elbows and knees were no longer on the raised platform though. I felt the new reality before I saw it. Or smelled it.

Hard earth. Green grass.

Suddenly I gasped in the air like a swimmer rising to the surface after being submerged too long. Still on my hands and knees I looked to my right and saw you grinning at the sky, lying straight on your back, bag clutched in your arms. Your eyes twitched over to me. We both began to laugh like we had in the lab. I rolled against you and you pushed me over, while keeping up the hysterical cackling. When we finally got our senses back, we sat up and looked around. This was the gentle treeless hill that I had aimed for, the place where mom and I had watched for Mack to appear. I looked up and saw a hawk circling. I peered all around and saw the monastery's tower beyond the trees, its windows clean, unboarded. The gardens, pump house, wishing well, gates, everything would be a short walk away. If it actually was June 15, 1994, then there'd be monks around, too, and we'd be trespassing.

I looked at you. "Your face is really red," I said, my voice loud in my head.

"So's yours. Like you had a facial. Hey, your hair is dry. How'd that happen?"

I ran my fingers through it. It wasn't just dry, it was all fly-away-staticky. And I swore it had grown thicker and longer, too. I pulled some strands in front of my nose; my hair was not quite the midnight black color I'd dyed it a week ago. I shrugged my shoulders at you and then noticed how different your hair looked. You'd gone blond the same day, but now your dark roots were obvious, like your hair had grown an inch. I decided not to mention it. "How do you feel? Everything in the right place?" You nodded. I took a deep breath again and stood up, not at all wobbly or dizzy or weak.

You stood too and lifted your arms to the sky, stretched, and arched and looked ready to let out a howl. "Laken, I can't believe we did it. This is awesome. I just want to shout."

"Don't make any loud noises," I said. "We don't know if the monks are around."

A thrill of expectation coursed through my veins as I said that. I didn't want to run into any religious hermits and at the same time I did, if only to prove that we had really done something super amazing.

I grabbed my bag and checked the contents. My phone wouldn't give the time or date and kept flashing an out of area message so I turned it off. We needed to get moving if we were going to search out Megan Hodges. It was a twenty-minute walk from here to town. I had a plan for locating her. I figured she'd head straight home, that is, where she thought she lived. Trouble was, her subdivision wouldn't even be developed for another ten years. If I were her, I'd then go to either the police station or the hospital. But I wasn't her. I knew from my research that she had grandparents in town; she'd head there. Of course they wouldn't know her and there was a chance that she wouldn't recognize them either if they were forty instead of seventy years old.

"Oh my gosh! I just thought of something."

"What?"

"Megan could run into her father. What if she recognizes him?"

"He'd be a teen, right? I've seen my dad's yearbook. Trust me, people change. A lot. Besides, so what if she thinks some teenager looks like her dad?"

You had a point, Skylar, but I wasn't sure. I didn't have any family pictures. No grandparents, no aunts or uncles. Our albums started when I was born.

"Well, anyway, I think we'll find her roaming around town. Probably dazed and confused. I should have listened to you and set the time machine back a day so we could catch her arriving on this hill."

"See, time travel makes you smarter."

I cocked my head and gave you my well-practiced glare. I noticed then that that little mole beside your eyebrow was gone. I reached up to touch my own hated dark mark that spoiled my chin. Nothing. No bump. Your eyes widened.

A bell sounded from somewhere in the monastery. Then a second ring. We counted together. Nine chimes. Nine o'clock in the morning.

"You know what?" You threw your bag over your shoulder, our moment of anxious wonder ended—why didn't certain things register? I dismissed the whole thing. "We should put our food and blankets in the pump house now so we don't have to hike all over carrying all this stuff."

"Not a bad idea."

"You know what would be really freaky?" you said as we walked like cats toward the pump house. "What if we do take the time machine again and go back to June 14, yesterday, and when we look in the pump house now, we find ourselves fast asleep."

"I hope not," I said, "because we would have barred the door. Then where do we sleep for the next twenty-six years?"

"Well, obviously somewhere that doesn't get disturbed since we made it back a second time."

I actually followed your line of thinking. Maybe time travel really had made me smarter. (And prettier?)

"Shh. There's a guy in the garden."

We waited only a few seconds until the man finished what he was doing, pruning I thought, and went back to the monastery.

Probably for breakfast. That sounded good. I was hungry. We'd eaten giant pretzels for lunch at the mall who knows how long ago. Well, a quarter of a century. I fished a couple of high calorie bars out of my bag and handed one to you. We finished them as we circled around to the pump house.

The rectangular building wasn't quite as dilapidated in the '90s as it was when I last saw it. My dad once told me it hadn't been used since the 1950s when the monastery got city water and sewer. That's what made the pump house the ideal place for hibernation—nobody would look through that dirty window or enter the building in decades. Especially since the monastery was soon to be closed and would sit empty until my parents bought it.

On my own I had tried to figure out other places to hibernate, but caves were damp and probably already claimed by wild animals, a crypt was out of the question, and unless something had been built specifically for this purpose how could a time traveler be sure he wouldn't be disturbed? I had thought of and dismissed sewers, cellars, morgues, and funeral homes. I even researched if our town had any elderly people who'd been home-bound for years. I thought that staying in their basement or attic could work, but I didn't find any possibilities. We had to use the little stone building, even if we found ourselves already sleeping there.

I looked up at the monastery. How different it appeared, more like a castle than a lab, severe in form, massive, and isolated. It looked impossible to knock down. The pump house featured the same cold stones, simple and unadorned, sequestered under the shadow of the larger building, but it somehow looked friendlier. We edged closer and crept along the side of the pump house. Luckily the door was on the sheltered end so if that monk came back to the garden we'd be out of sight.

I tried the knob, praying that it would open easily. I didn't really expect to see ourselves asleep inside like you described, but apparently my thumping heart considered it a possibility. The knob turned stiffly and I pushed. You put one hand on it, too, and shoved. The door scraped along the concrete floor letting the daylight inch across the darkness. Remember?

Empty. At least empty of any sleeping bodies. There were thick iron pipes erupting through the cement that crossed over a square manhole cover then attached to what looked like a serious industrial-sized pump. The pump took up at least a third of the space, tattooed with rust and covered in cobwebs. The place was filthy and clearly home to spiders and mice, judging by the small black droppings all around the pump. How on earth were we going to sleep in there?

"Dibs on the top bunk," you whispered. That drew my eyes up. Along the wall across from the solitary high window hung four wooden cots. "I'll bet they used to send the bad monks out here for punishment."

"I doubt it," I whispered back. "More likely they've been stored here and forgotten. Lucky for us." I stepped all the way in and handed you my bag because no way was I going to set it on the floor. I reached up and jiggled one of the cots off a long nail that protruded from the roof beam. I sputtered and blew at the dust that rained down as the cot dropped into my arms. Neither of us could keep from saying 'eew,' but at least we managed not to scream when a mouse skeleton fell from the beam.

"I don't know about this, Laken. Maybe we should look for someplace else."

"This is our best bet." I set up the cot and tested it. It was surprisingly sturdy and not uncomfortable, though a bit narrow. I shoved it under the window and you set both our bags on it. You retrieved the second and third cot and set them up. We barely had any space left, but that didn't really matter.

The light that filtered in through the half open door darkened abruptly and my heart skipped a beat as if my own shadow had crossed over me.

"Did you hear that?" you whispered.

"It was just a cloud," I said. "You can't hear a cloud. Let's lighten our bags and hit the trail."

The truth was I did hear something, Sky. When I was little my dad used to tell me bedtime stories about a beautiful queen named Emily, same name as my mom, who was searching for her lost princess daughter, Laken, that was me. Every time he got to the part where the queen would call out my name, my mom would sing out the same two notes from another room: "Laaaa-ken." I swear that's what I heard coming from outside the gray stone pump house. But I have a good imagination and maybe it was made better by time travel.

Chapter 8

We found the trail that led through the back part of the twenty acres of private Benedictine property. I knew these woods as well as I knew my way around school, and even though the trees were different in '94 there was no mistaking the remains of a junked car at the end of a two-track lane. I took a moment to analyze the car's condition. Stripped of tires, radio, and whatever valuable parts some thief absolutely had to have, the car still sported its ripped seats which oozed gray matted stuffing. The car even had paint on the hood. It was an oxidized frame in my day, but now I could see it had once been red.

"We go that way," I said. I pointed toward where I was positive the main road would be and turned to look back at where we came from. "When we come back with Megan, remember we keep angling to the right, past the rusted car. We won't get lost, even if it's dark."

I caught a glimpse of trepidation on your face. I knew about your fear of the dark and was glad I had the flashlight app on my phone. It might take us longer than expected to find Megan. I wasn't exactly afraid of the dark, but I didn't want to be going through the woods at midnight, either.

I swatted at a mosquito and hoped that black fly season was over.

It didn't feel right to chatter on about boys and music and school the way we usually would. We walked in silence. I for one was totally amazed at the enormity of our expedition. My heart hadn't stopped tripping and dancing since we arrived. The morning seemed clearer and brighter as if the sun were a younger star shining down with more light and enthusiasm than it would in the next century. The air however felt heavy, damp, and cold. Yet I was feverishly warm. That was the second aftereffect. Like the first thing, I ignored it too.

Our little town looked the same and you echoed my thoughts on that out loud.

"Looks the same. If we hadn't just come from the monastery, I wouldn't know what year it was."

"Yeah, it does look the same at first glance, but see down there?" I pointed down the right side of the street, past Ray's Jewelers and the pharmacy. "The dollar store is open. I used to go in there all the time, but it closed last summer."

"Let's go in. We've got money."

I disregarded your suggestion and stood stock still. The driver of the car that stopped for the light was staring at me with the oddest expression. It was a lady, older than my mom, and not familiar looking at all. I linked my arm with yours and forcefully dragged you across the road, weaving on the crosswalk closer to the hood of the car. I got a good look at the woman and she stared at me, too. Her mouth hung open for too long then her fingers rose next to her cheek and she gave me an acknowledging wave. I had no idea who the heck she was, but some memory tickled my brain. Or maybe it was déjà vu.

The light changed and a truck honked when she didn't get going right away. I dropped your arm and watched her drive off. My heart thumped with dread.

"Who was that? Do you know her?" You pushed me toward a bench. "Sit down. You look like you've seen a ghost."

"No. Nobody I know. I don't think—" That was the last thing I remembered saying. No kidding, I didn't think another thought the rest of the day. I spoke, I walked, and apparently we followed my plan to locate Megan, but I had a blackout that put me on autopilot. PTSD. Post time-travel stress disorder.

When I finally came out of it we were sitting in the Big Boy restaurant feasting on burgers and fries and milkshakes. The music coming over the speakers was loud in my head and I was seeing double, hearing double, too … *how can you stay away, stay away, away so long, away so long … give me a reason, give me a reason.*

I mentally cursed when my eyes zeroed in on the wall clock. It was nearly seven o'clock. I'd missed the whole day.

"What's the matter, Laken? You're doing it again."

"Doing what?"

"Zoning out. I swear time-traveling turned you into a zombie." You slurped your chocolate shake. "Who are you staring at?" You swiveled your head around. "Oh my gosh, it's that woman again."

I was already looking over your shoulder. Beyond the salad bar and past the row of fake plants that same woman sat in the solarium part of the restaurant. She rose, left a tip, and walked toward us instead of toward the cashier.

"Hello, Laken. It is you, isn't it? You've colored your hair. I like it."

I struggled just to focus on her face.

"May I sit down?"

I glanced at you and gestured with my head for you to slide over. But you didn't. The woman slipped into the booth next to you without even looking at you. Her eyes kept drilling into me. I would have been totally freaked out and terrified if she were a man. Think rapist, murderer, psycho. Something in her expression said she knew more about bad stuff than anyone should.

And then it hit me who she was.

"Shelly Ayers." I flicked my eyes to you and saw the wheels turning in your head. You were probably doing the math like I was. I sent Shelly to 1963 when she was seventeen. She'd be late forties in '94. "You've changed."

"A few pounds, a few wrinkles."

"Did you get to see the Beatles?"

She measured my question before answering. "No, Laken, I didn't."

I had the sudden urge to tell her that I knew when she was going to die, but our meeting was awkward enough. "Too bad," I said. "I know you wanted to. At least you got to grow up in the '60s. It wasn't so bad, was it? Everything turned out all right for you, right?" She nodded slowly like she was remembering, a slight curl raised the corner of her lips. Inwardly I was stunned that we were talking, and I was elated for her because she seemed fine, but there was another emotion flooding to the surface that I couldn't identify. Anxiety, maybe, like I'd forgotten something really important.

"What are you doing here?" she asked, her eyes still probing mine.

"Uh, my best friend, Skylar, came with me to look for a girl I sent to this year." I motioned toward you and I saw that you held your hand half-ready to finger wave if Shelly turned toward you, but Shelly gave a startled jump instead as if she only just then realized she was sitting next to someone. She stared down at your bag that took up all the space between the two of you.

She turned her attention back to me after smiling over your head and ignoring your little finger wave. "What girl?"

"Oh, my gosh. Maybe you could help us. Her name is Megan Hodges and I put her in the time machine the same way I did for you, but I sent her to June 15, 1994. That is today, right? We weren't positive. My phone doesn't work."

Shelly glanced at her watch. It was gold with diamonds glittering up the band. "Yes, that's today's date."

"Thank goodness. Megan has leukemia, I think. Her sister died a month ago. Well, actually she isn't even born yet." My laugh sounded maniacal even to my ears. The waitress looked my way. "Anyway, I thought Megan was abused, like you were. Only now I think she wasn't, so I need to find her and take her back to our time so she can get medical help."

Shelly didn't have any trouble following my story. If I remembered correctly she already had her foundation for abused kids up and running. She understood this subject.

The waitress came over then and asked us if we wanted anything else. She left the bill on the table and Shelly picked it up. She smiled. "I'll get this for you."

"Thanks. That's so nice of you, but you don't have to. We have plenty of money."

"No problem. Now, how can I help you find this Megan?"

Good question. "Well, since it's so late, maybe we could split up and check the hospital, the shelter, and the police station."

You spoke up at last. "We already did those, Lake. Are you still spaced out?"

"No. Scratch that. We haven't gone looking for her grandparents yet, have we, Sky?" You nodded and Shelly cocked her head and frowned at me. Then she reached across and patted my hand.

"Megan will be all right. Don't worry. These things always work out." A muffled ring came from her purse and she said "Excuse me," and took the call. A few seconds later she leaned forward and said, "I'm sorry, Laken, I have an emergency. I have to go. Do you have a way to get home?"

I nodded rather than explain to her about the hibernation pills. Pills could mean something entirely different to someone who lived through the '60s.

"Another time machine?" she asked, her face lifting gently in an understanding smile.

"No, not a time machine."

"That's good. Well," she stood up and waved the bill at me, "have a good evening. Take care of yourself."

I watched her walk to the cashier and experienced a wave of nausea. I swallowed hard. The last thing I wanted was to throw up all the calories I'd need to sleep.

"Laken?" Your voice sounded far away, as distant as the words to the song I recognized coming through the speakers.

"What?" I shook off the image of the suicidal singers.

"I don't feel so good. And I'm scared. Let's go back to the pump house before it gets dark."

Chapter 9

I didn't like her." You threw your bag on the cot and let loose with a few potty-mouth words as soon as we sneaked into the pump house. You'd acted upset the entire walk back through the woods, even kicked at the rusted car like it was to blame for something. "That woman, that Shelly whatever, wouldn't even make eye contact with me. You know, sociopaths don't make eye contact."

"Shh, don't get so upset. I'm positive that Shelly Ayers is not a sociopath." I threw in a few curse words of my own to get my point across.

"She didn't even help us."

"She paid our check."

"Big deal."

"Well, if I needed help she's who I'd go to. Sky, what's really wrong?"

"I don't know." You moved your bag to the foot of the cot and sat down. "I'm scared. It'll be dark soon. I want to go home … see my parents … have a date with a hot guy next week, not next century."

"All right, all right. Let's finish eating these bars and figure out the exact number of pills we need to take." I took off the lake and sky pendant and handed it to you. "Your turn."

You calmed down then. You clasped the chain behind your neck and fingered the design. Then you searched for a pen in your purse and started scribbling on the back of a receipt. You mumbled your way through figuring out the years and months and days, how many days left after June 15 of this year, how many days from January first of 2020 to the day we left. After you double checked your math you told me you needed to add in seven days for leap years. I never would have thought of that. Then you divided up the pills according to your calculations. Smart, smart, smart. I was so lucky you came with me even if we didn't find Megan. I started thinking then that when we got back, I'd convince you to go again and then we'd do it your way and arrive yesterday, and catch Megan this morning. But right away I thought no, that couldn't work, or we would have found ourselves sleeping here already.

"What's the matter, Laken? You're zoning out again."

"I can't even … crap … I know why we couldn't find her in town. She's got to be right here. She may even have arrived *after* us. She probably knocked on the monastery door. What do you want to bet she's tucked snugly in a bed inside the monastery?"

We both mulled over my brilliant deduction for a few seconds. "You might be right. We could at least peek in the windows and see if she's in there."

I spread out the Mylar blankets then, one on each cot. You counted out more pills for Megan and placed the pills and a bottle of water on each blanket. It was odd how we were sure we'd find her with the monks. Then I caught myself from laughing too loud. "Monks in the cell now; monkeys in the cell in our time."

You embellished your signature eye roll with a weak laugh.

***

There were candles lit inside the monastery. We couldn't go to the back door because the garden monk had closed and locked the gate. We could have climbed it because there was no razor wire in '94, but we decided to chance knocking on the front door instead. No one answered our shy taps. We stood there raising our eyebrows at each other until you finally checked the door knob. It was unlocked. We let ourselves in and turned left into the base of the tower. Apparently it was used as a small-scale chapel. The walls were covered with tapestries of Persian silk— one hundred percent silk, according to the tag that you read in whispered tones. They glowed with golden threads that shimmered in the light of a vast number of candles. Over the altar, beneath a canopy of purple velvet, loomed a full-length portrait of Christ, the shepherd. His eyes fixed on me and my stomach twisted in hypocritical grief.

"This feels backwards," you said, "like we've gone through the looking-glass. Shouldn't the bedroom cells, Mack's and Reese's rooms, be through that hallway?"

I agreed. It did feel odd, but then I wasn't even walking yet when my parents remodeled this place; I'd never seen the original floor plan.

"Shh. Stay close."

I led you past the table that held the most candles. The smoke curled along the stone wall; the gentle heat kissed my cheek and arm. The candles were not the scented kind yet they gave off a smell that troubled me, as if a bad memory was hiding in the wax, unformed. I pushed open the heavy door and we slipped out. When it closed soundlessly it took a moment for our eyes to adjust. There was barely enough light coming through the cracks along the frame to see that the hallway was empty. We tip-toed toward the other end.

The hallway looked unchanged except that every solid oak bedroom door, set back in its original alcove, was windowless.

I nearly jumped straight up when you tapped my shoulder. You whispered, "I think we should go back outside and knock again. Let's do this right."

I had to admit the thought of opening the wrong door and confronting a grown man instead of Megan was more than a little terrifying, even if the man was a peaceful, celibate monk. We were, after all, trespassing. I was about to whisper back when the second to last door creaked opened. The cell—that in a couple of decades would house a chimpanzee—now gave off the shadow of a much larger ape. Instead of pressing ourselves into the nearest alcove we froze.

A robed figure emerged carrying a candle in an old-fashioned holder. The quivering flame danced across the bruised face of Megan Hodges, framed not by a robe as I had first thought, but by the hood on the windbreaker I'd laid on her stomach before setting the time machine, oh about six months ago. When she began to walk toward us she didn't seem to notice us at first.

"Is that her?" Your hoarse whisper begged Megan to see us.

She held the candle aloft and strained to peer into the gloom. I was afraid she was poised to scream so I hurried to assure her we were friendly. "Megan, it's me. It's Laken. Are you all right?"

"Laken? My head still hurts. I was coming to look for you. Do you have any aspirin?" She lifted her other hand to her forehead where the bruise and cut she received the night of the party looked worse in the unsteady candlelight.

I nudged you and gave you a knowing look. To Megan this was still the night I brought her here. She wobbled closer and I grabbed the candle out of her hand.

"Oh," she said, putting her arm on mine for balance, "I couldn't find the light switch. The candle and matches were on the windowsill."

Though she spoke in a low voice it was loud enough to alert someone. I hoped she'd pick up on the fact I was whispering. "I have aspirin, Megan, and something stronger, too. Can you walk by yourself? Here, take my arm."

I linked my arm in hers and you walked on her other side. We shuffled back to the tower where I set the candle down. We went out the front entry and retraced our route. Megan was barefoot, but she didn't complain. Undoubtedly she still had some illegal drugs in her system. I began to think that maybe she only recently arrived. It could be that my coordinates were a number off and I sent her to the very cell she just came out of. Maybe the monks didn't even know she was here.

We circled around outside and I looked up at the third floor. Candlelight flickered there, too, and shadows swayed. I imagined three or four men chanting quiet prayers, but I couldn't really hear anything.

"Are we going back to the party? Where's your car?"

"No, the party's over." I chanced talking more normally. "My friend Skylar is here and we're going to get you home."

Megan stumbled then and we caught her. "I don't have my shoes. My shoes," she laughed, "are stuck. It was so funny." I couldn't make sense of what she was saying. Maybe a person shouldn't time-travel while drunk or stoned.

I switched on my cell phone and lit our way into the pump house. Megan collapsed onto the middle cot and sent a couple of pills flying, but the rest were trapped under her. You scrambled to catch the two sizable pills that rolled toward the floor openings under the pipes. You scraped yourself, didn't you? And that's when you grunted like Mack. It wasn't funny. At least you snared twenty years' worth of encapsulated hibernation with the quickest swipe of your hand.

Debra Chapoton

"Megan, sit up," I said, setting my phone on the edge of my cot. It was a struggle to get her upright. "Here, you have to eat these." I unwrapped a number of bars and held them in front of her face.

"Oh, I'm starving. Thanks so much." She perked up enough to take each offered bar and, more quickly than I expected, she devoured them one after another.

I rescued the rest of Megan's sleep agent from where they rolled against her thigh on the cot. I pointed at the pills and mouthed '*she's first.*' You nodded back. I didn't know how long before the hibernation would begin so it was a good plan to make Megan go first.

"How do you feel?" you asked her, but Megan ignored your question and kept munching. I have a theory why she ignored you and why Shelly did too in the restaurant. I'll get to that later.

When she finally swallowed she asked, "Where are we, Laken?"

"Someplace safe. Don't worry. I'll have you home before you know it."

"I have to go to the hospital. I have to see my sister."

You and I exchanged one of those sympathetic looks and I cleared my throat before I lied. "I'll take you straight to the hospital. Promise. Here, take these pills. Wash them down with this water."

If I thought it was easy sending her off in the time machine, sending her into a catatonic sleep was twice as simple. She downed the last pill and drank half of a second bottle of water.

"I'm kind of sleepy," she slurred.

"You can take a little nap if you want," I said. "Stretch out and I'll cover you with this blanket."

68

I helped Megan to her feet so we could get the blanket around her. We cocooned her up like a burrito and eased her back onto the cot. My phone's light dimmed and flickered, signaling us to hurry up.

"She's out," you said.

"Yup. Hopefully for twenty-six years. I hope she doesn't wake up first." I fussed with tucking the blanket around her bare feet.

"She won't. I gave her one extra day's worth. Unless her metabolism is different or she weighs a lot more, and I don't think she does, she'll sleep longer than we will." You gave me the most peculiar look then and it crossed my mind to compare the number and sizes of the pills that were yours and mine, but I dropped that suspicion as soon as I thought it. You know when you can trust someone with your life. I trusted you, Skylar.

"We need to bar the door somehow, Sky. Any suggestions?"

"The fourth cot." You reached up and unhooked the remaining cot and assembled it. Then you wedged it between the door and the ends of our cots. There was no space left in the pump house. You reached over the cot and tried to pull the door open, but the cot's frame held fast and the door wasn't going to budge.

We sat on our little beds, finished our protein bars, and gulped my mother's super sedatives without gagging. My phone was still emitting adequate light as we bundled ourselves up in the Mylar blankets. I for one got as cozy as I could, tucking and re-tucking the edges of the thin silver material around myself, hoping I'd fall asleep before the light died out. I didn't expect to dream, but before I completely passed out I sensed a pushing movement at my feet, like someone was ramming the door and that movement was jostling my cot. I heard you sigh and then for

69

sure I had a dream because my mother's voice faintly echoed in my ear: "Laa-ken!" and I couldn't move.

Chapter 10

Time Machine Date: 2020 Again

There was something exceptional about dreaming during a sleep that beat out Rip Van Winkle's twenty year nap. If there's such a thing as a calm nightmare that's what I had. Over and over I dreamed of waking up and finding myself in a coffin, or finding you and Megan as skinless, rotting skeletons, or finding myself being carried high on the shoulders of several tall monks who intended to throw me into a bottomless well. The good part of that revolving nightmare was that I was never afraid. A gentle voice repeated my name, assured me I was fine, and told me not to worry. It sounded vaguely like my own voice or my mother's.

From time to time, I felt that I was on the verge of waking. That's when the nightmares would abate for a while. I shivered and dreamed of snow. I was aware that I was sleeping, if that was possible. Perhaps it was a side effect of the sleep agent, but I was happy in my head. Content to sleep for twenty-six plus years.

Waking up was almost impossible.

The first thing I realized was that my eyelids were crusty and glued shut. I tried to raise my hand to my face but I had to struggle against the blanket. It was tucked so tightly that both my arms were pinned down. I grunted, forced my eyes open, and stared at the old oak beams in the ceiling. It took a moment to focus on the different details; the light coming through the dirty window was meager, but enough to illuminate the pump house.

I turned my head and saw Megan's pale face tilted toward me. She was still wrapped tightly, but the hood on her windbreaker was tattered as if Cinderella's mice had pulled the threads out one by one.

I watched her for signs of breathing and noticed the slowest rise of her chest. My own breathing remained equally shallow. I tried opening my mouth to suck in a deeper breath, but coughed instead. My tongue had ridges; it had conformed to the shape of my teeth, sinking into the indentations between tooth and gum. There wasn't enough moisture in my mouth to spit if I wanted to.

I tried again to move my arms and wormed one hand out. I wiped at my face and picked at the gunk crusted around my nose, mouth, and eyes. I must have lain there for ten minutes after I freed my other hand, just grooming my face, brushing off flakes of I-don't-know-what that had dried to my cheeks. I blinked my eyes over and over until they watered, ran my fingers through my hair, and itched my ears.

I couldn't see you because Megan was between us. I looked over at Megan again. Her face looked more like a mask to me now that my eyes were clear and more light was filtering in from a vent in the gable.

I cleared my throat and whispered, "Megan? Sky?" I tried again louder, my voice squeaky and scratched. "Skylar? Are you awake?" The sounds I made were more like Velcro than words; I probably only thought I was speaking.

I wanted to rise up to a sitting position, but so far I could only use my arms. I lifted my head and looked down the cot toward the door. The fourth cot no longer braced the door closed. It lay crippled on its side. Anyone could come along and push the door wide into the opening it left. That thought was the scare I needed to shoot some primal adrenaline through my body. My heart skittered, my legs twitched, my feet grew hot. I struggled to sit up, moved my legs over the edge of the cot, and unwrapped myself from the Mylar. My head spun; I'd never felt so dizzy. Finally my mouth had enough saliva so I could do more than croak.

I looked at your cot and gasped. "Sky! Where are you?"

Your blanket lay neatly folded, your bag gone.

A sudden twitch of Megan's body drew my attention to her. I was super glad I wasn't alone with a dead girl. Her head moved slowly maybe a half an inch and revealed a black beetle nestled in the fold of her neck. I bent forward to brush it away, but the movement amplified how lightheaded I was and I stopped, waited a second then tried again. The beetle scuttled aside when my fingers touched her hair. It burrowed underneath her clothes and I gave up. Megan's half bottle of water lay on its side under her cot. I tapped it with an outstretched foot and realized that I couldn't hear any sounds, not the crinkle of plastic as my shoe hit it and not the light sound it should have made as it rolled my way. It took what little strength I had to unscrew the cap and lift the dusty plastic to my lips.

I tasted nothing. The water slipped easily down my throat and after a minute or two the woozy feeling passed and I could stand up, but still I heard zero sounds.

I wondered where in the world you were.

My once beautiful bag was hanging from the hook that the cots had hung from. That wasn't where I'd left it. It looked old and tattered. I remembered leaving my phone on with the flashlight feature dimming as we fell asleep. I sat back down and felt beneath my cot keeping my hand just above the cold concrete. The phone I found was dusty, dingy, and crushed. How the heck did it get crushed? Well, I couldn't have known why then, but I know why now. It'll be obvious as you read all of this letter—by the way, Sky, I'm still apologizing. Please know that.

Anyway, I sat there a while and stared at the floor. I don't know for how long, but it was long enough for my hearing to return. First, I noticed Megan's breathing, ragged and not rhythmic at all. Then it was the weather outside that invaded my head. I listened to the wind, the rain, the thumps of sticks and acorns pelting the roof.

When the squall passed, I decided to leave the pump house and search for you, but first I wanted my bag. It was tricky to step over Megan and get to the beam and even trickier to release the bag from high on the hook. When it flipped free it fell smack onto my face and then slid through my weakened hands. I gasped as I saw all the skin that fell away from my arms.

I was standing there in shock when I heard a new sound. The door opened, bumped hard against the fourth cot's wooden slats, and closed behind you.

"You're up," you said. Your voice sounded strong. You glanced from me to Megan. "She'll be out a little longer."

My first words were unintelligible. I coughed and tried again. "Where have you been? What day is it?"

"You're not going to believe it, Laken."

You crawled across your cot and met me at the beam, making me wait ten whole seconds for what I wasn't going to believe. You said, "It's exactly an hour before I first came here with you. I mean, it's April 4th, 2020. We—the original you and me—are at the drug store right now, looking at funny birthday cards."

You touched the lake and sky pendant and added, "And buying stuff. We're going to show up here in a bit and go in the time machine."

You started speaking faster than I could take it in. "So we can follow ourselves back into the lab, unlock poor Mack's door, and figure out where we want to dump Megan."

"Dump Megan?"

"You're still a little blurry, aren't you? I'm sorry, you need some more time. I woke up yesterday and it took me a few hours to get normal. Thank goodness I knew my way around the lab. A little food, a shower, fresh clothes. I felt normal in no time. It was lonely though. I kept coming back to check on you two. It was a long, lonely night. Spooky."

I sank to the floor and let your whirl of words spin around in my head. Here my skin was falling off me like in a zombie movie and you were chattering on as if we hadn't just defied the laws of nature.

"Eat a protein bar, Laken. You'll feel better." You pulled one out of your pocket, a fresh one.

It had no appeal, but you were probably right. I unwrapped the bar. By the second bite I had something to say.

"How'd you get into the lab? It should have been locked."

"Well, it was and it wasn't. Listen to this. I checked the well first and the brick with the keys wasn't there so then I went to the gate, which was latched and locked. I could see a car inside, not yours, and figured it wasn't the right day. You were right about this place being secure. I walked around and couldn't peek in any windows or anything so I went to the front door and knocked."

I finished the bar despite its muddy taste, so unlike what I remembered, and started rubbing the shreds of skin off my arms as I listened.

"And nobody answered," we said together.

"How'd you know?" You scrunched your face up and I noticed how smooth your skin looked.

"The car was dark blue, wasn't it?" My parents would have been working here before they took off for one of their retreats.

"Yeah, navy. Four doors."

"My parents were working in the lab. Dad puts the speakers on loud and my mom wears a headset. They have opposite tastes in music. They wouldn't hear a bomb go off."

"Yeah, well I figured they had to come out sooner or later so I sat down and waited. I was pretty weak after trekking around the building. I didn't hear the car start up. All of a sudden it was passing by the front and I didn't have a chance to shout. There was no way I was strong enough to walk to town and my clothes were literally falling off me. My skin too."

"You look all right now."

"Thanks. So anyway, I started to come back to the pump house to see if you were awake yet. On the way I noticed that the gate was ajar so I thought they were coming right back. Instead of checking on you I went in and, you'll never guess, that super secure double-locked back door was also wide open."

Something didn't add up. Of all the times to not lock their precious lab my parents had chosen the very day we needed it unlocked and then they just went off on one of their over-nighters?

"Wide open?" I didn't understand. I put my palms against my temples and squeezed, let my fingernails scrape through my hairline, and drew them back out, clumps of hair following. "Oh!"

"Don't worry. You'll be fine once you shower. I was shocked when I looked in the mirror, but all the dead cells will slough off."

I hoped so. I looked at the long and short strands of hair in my hands and pulled them off my fingers. "Why aren't my fingernails six feet long?"

"I wondered that, too." You turned your hands toward me and back again. Your nails were short, maybe shorter than when we left. "I was hoping to have hair down to my butt too, but I still have most of my bleached-blond hair. And the blue streak." You shook your head twice and I couldn't tell any difference other than the dark roots I noticed after we first time-traveled.

A groan from Megan made both of us look over.

"She's getting close to waking," you said. "We need to figure this out before ... uh ... before your car rolls up with us in it and the gate's not locked. That would make a paradox, right?"

It felt like my brain knocked the top of my skull when I nodded. But that was the last bad side effect. Well, for a while. I let you take the lead as we walked to the lab. Some of the people we passed were wearing surgery masks. Weird.

Chapter 11

It was odd to find the gates and doors open, my car not there, and the lab looking the same and yet not the same. The mice cages needed cleaning almost as much as I did. You said you'd take care of it while I showered and changed. I don't think I thanked you then, but thanks for doing that, Sky.

Mack huffed and puffed at me when I walked by his cell, but he didn't open his door—the door that I, in a little while, was going to lock, in what to my muddled mind was both my past and my future.

I picked out some ordinary clothes from the rack in the supply room and held them away from myself as I walked to the bathroom. There I stripped off my old things. It was positively disgusting how gunked up my clothes were. Bits of me clung in patches to the insides of my jeans and shirt. My bra and panties were indescribable. I didn't dare look in the mirror. I stuffed everything into the waste container and turned the shower on.

You were right about how the shower would wash twenty odd years of dead flesh down the drain. At first, I only let the water trickle on my hands and watched the rivulets of grime stream toward the drain. Then I turned it on full blast, stepped under the shower head, and closed my eyes. I scrubbed and soaped and shampooed four times then let the hot water and steam finish the job. When I dried off and looked in the mirror my skin glowed. Scrutinizing myself, I seemed smaller, shorter maybe, but better proportioned than before. Or maybe that was wishful thinking on my part and selfish reflecting on the part of the mirror. Anyway, I was relieved. More of my strength had returned and I couldn't feel any other bad aftereffects from our two modes of time travel.

I dressed and walked out to find you playing with the same blue-streaked mouse you were going to meet for the first time in a little while.

"So," you said, putting him back into the clean cage, "we need to get Megan to the hospital. It'd probably be best if we do it before she wakes up. I gave her an extra day's pill, you know."

I nodded absently. I stared at the lake and sky pendant around your neck. The silver chain and glass artwork were undiminished by time. Like our friendship. I stared at you and wondered why we'd gotten so close. It wasn't just our identical interests in science and shopping and boys, not necessarily in that order, that made us best friends. We trusted one another implicitly. But why? I had no doubt that you'd never betray this secret.

"Earth to Laken. What is it? What are you thinking? Is it your turn to wear this again?" You reached for the pendant's clasp. "I suppose that's fair. I've had it now for, oh, a quarter of a century." You laughed and stepped behind me, pulled my still damp hair out of the way, and fastened the chain.

"There's something I need to tell you, Sky." It bothered me to keep drip-feeding you bits of information and watching your reaction.

"What?"

I bit my lip. "Sometimes time travel involves, um," I wasn't sure which word to use—murder, manslaughter, unfortunate mishaps—I settled on "accidental death."

You let slip a nervous chuckle. "So? You're saying that we better get Megan to the hospital as soon as the other you and the other me get in the time machine, right? That shouldn't be a problem. We could call an ambulance."

I sighed and did a 'yes and no' head roll. "You've heard all the stories of decomposed bodies found in the last forty or fifty years, right? And all of the missing girls more recently?"

You clutched at where the pendant no longer hung near your heart. I had the eerie feeling that I'd already explained this to you. Maybe I had because you said, "There were no kidnappers or serial killers, were there? It was the time machine." Your eyes widened and you looked down the hall toward the tower. "But—"

"I really thought I was doing good deeds. I'd do it all over again, too."

"Do what, exactly?"

"Well, send them back. You know; I've already explained … that I helped six girls. But I've had this ugly feeling that maybe, maybe, my coordinates weren't right. To tell you the truth, I added six feet of elevation to our time jump and we landed perfectly on the hill. Remember? I thought we'd fall six feet, but we didn't. That means I might have sent some girls to their graves. And I don't mean symbolically."

I didn't breathe. The frozen look on your face was more frightening than the agonizing death I imagined my victims endured.

"Laken. Oh, Laken, I won't believe it. That lady was alive. And Megan wasn't buried."

I dropped my head enough to look up at you like an innocent puppy. It was the same pleading look I'd give my mom whenever I wanted her to believe a lie, though my mom never fell for it. You put your arm around me, told me again that you didn't believe I'd done anything wrong, and reminded me that we needed to get out of the lab soon.

That was when the back lab door slammed. We'd left the gate and the door open an inch because we had no keys. My first thought was my dad was here, or both my parents. Then we heard a raspy groan, like sandpaper trying to form words.

"Megan?"

You bolted toward the hallway, but I was slower.

I stopped as soon as I saw her. She stumbled then crumpled against the wall. You squatted down and gently pushed some hair away from her eyes, eyes that Megan had already rubbed vigorously. I was horrified. Her face, which looked like a mask before, had deep cracks around her mouth. Trickles of blood seeped from both eyes, her nose, her mouth.

"Did I look like that?" I took a few steps closer.

You put your arm around Megan and tried to lift her up.

"You were almost as bad, Laken, but not this bloody."

Your effort was wasted; it would take both of us in our diluted conditions to support Megan. For the tiniest instant I imagined you in ten years as a veterinarian, trying to gather a long-legged foal in your arms. You slipped your left arm under Megan's knees.

"What do you think you're doing? Let me help." I bent down on the other side and together we provided enough leverage to get her upright. Her head lolled over toward my shoulder and all I could think of was how clean I was and how rotting Megan was. Wisps of her hair brushed my cheek like fairy hands, grasping, tickling.

We put her in the first chair we came to in the lab and I rubbed my cheek against my shoulder hoping to brush off any of Megan's foul flesh. I caught her reflection and mine in the blank computer screen. Megan did too. She cried out with the most pathetic sound ever and kept repeating a chant that sounded like *'send the beast to hell.'* Yes, that was exactly what she said. Do you remember?

"It's all right, Megan. You'll be fine in a little while." I started to give her a soothing pat with my hand then thought better of it.

Her body went incredibly limp all of a sudden. She slipped from the chair to the floor before either of us could stop her. In my fight against sudden hysteria I wanted to say 'good snake impression' and laugh, but you grabbed my hand and squeezed hard so instead of laughing I cried. We knew before we checked her pulse that Megan was dead.

Chapter 12

What did we do with a dead body while a storm brewed outside, the lights actually flickered, and the minutes ticked closer to the moment when my car would drive up? You would have thought we'd discussed the subject before. Because in less than five minutes of rational, scientific debate we settled on burying Megan, time machine style, in the hill out back. It sounded cold and callous, but really it was the best thing for everyone. Does this sound familiar?

Mack made agitated chimpanzee howls when we dragged Megan down the hall, past his cell. The steps were the worst. Her toes smacked every stair tread with a dull thump. It was heartbreaking.

The third floor didn't spook you this time, but I was disturbed by the ethereal, ghostlike atmosphere in the tower room. The light from the hall glowed amid the shadows that played on the windows. There was an eerie silence, except for the snapping sound the machine was making, more like a time bomb ticking than a car engine cooling down. I got the lights on without relinquishing my hold around Megan's waist. I feared holding her too tightly as much as I feared giving the burden completely to you.

"Must have been the leukemia," I muttered.

"We should have left her in '94. She could've gotten medical help." You helped me lift her onto the platform. At least, I *thought* you did. She seemed awfully heavy, like you weren't helping at all. The top layer of Megan's arm peeled off as I arranged her body. I could see an area of fresh, pale skin, but there were also blotches of bluish spots. The flesh that had rotted away lay clumped between her elbow and the bed. It would all be transported into the ground. Mercifully. Along with the black beetle that crawled out of her sleeve.

You stepped back to the door and watched me go to the machine's controls. I set the date to match the wall clock, April 4. I had a déjà vu moment and then I set the hill's coordinates, minus six feet. I looked over at you, Sky, and waited for you to nod. There was a barely concealed fear that haunted your eyes and a tremor in your hands. But we were in this together. The biggest secret ever. Lake and Sky. Sky and Laken.

I hit the switch. And three, two, one, Megan and all gory trace of her vanished. Watching her disappear was different from the first time. There was no sizzling thrill. Just a numbness. And I think the room wobbled. The walls and floor were bathed in amber light.

You began to cry. We hugged and you shuddered and I held you up. There was a thin line between energizing terror and death. We gave up five minutes of precious time to grieve over Megan, a girl I hardly knew and who you knew even less. Then, while the rain took a break, we had to do several things to avoid creating a paradox … cuz it sure seemed like a paradox *did* have something to do with the death toll.

Twenty minutes later you hid in the bedroom cell where seven mice with red stripes hibernated in cages, right across from Mack's room.

And I went outside and watched from the corner of the pump house as my car came to the gate and my arm slipped out the window holding the brick and keys. I caught a glimpse of you in the passenger seat and then my car went through the gate. I saw myself park the car and I spied on myself as I—my body anyway—came back and my hand wedged a stick in the gate and

I disappeared into the lab with you—or rather, with a girl who looked almost the same as you. But not quite.

The rain began to fall once more and I ducked into the pump house to wait until the sun came out again. I knew I didn't need to bar the door, but I couldn't help myself. I lodged two cots against the door, just in case that in this new reality a different me decided to put the brick of keys in the well and then yield to the temptation to check the pump house. For a brief passing moment that thought was quite exhilarating. A few seconds and one wrong move and we'd all close in on a fatal paradox.

A slow chill of weariness settled into my bones and I sat on the cot, wrapped myself again in the Mylar blanket and waited, trusting that my original self would complete the tasks exactly as I remembered. Of course, as I'm writing this now I realize that memories are not absolute. Anyway, my mind wandered into a fog of regret. I had blanked out for several hours when we searched for Megan in '94 and I was sure that the same thing was happening again only this time I was fully aware of time passing as I sat in the pump house. Rough rectangles of light at the periphery of my vision begged to be noticed, but I concentrated on the bleak darkness of the pump house's interior, until I couldn't help it any longer. My gaze detoured to the trapdoor under the ancient pump's pipes, while my thoughts focused on why the other Sky—the original you—looked slightly different to me.

The absence of lucid thought and the struggle to remember certain things started to get to me. Names and events escaped me. I couldn't think of Megan's last name. I couldn't visualize Shelly Ayer's grown-up face. I knew I'd seen the rusted car, but I sensed there was some hidden meaning in it that was vitally important. Trivial details outweighed crucial facts that were on the tip of my tongue, the edge of my remembrance. Unquestionably such a crazy state of mind was another consequence of time travel or maybe of hibernation. I closed my eyes and tried to center myself, tried to think happy thoughts, tried to feel … right.

A deluge of memories barrel-rolled behind my closed lids and chased away whatever happy recollections I might have had. Instead I remembered my tenth birthday, when a girl in my class gave everyone the chicken pox and no one came to my party; when I was twelve and got my first period and Shelly told all the boys to stare at my butt; when I started ninth grade and had a crush on Bryan Hage and Ciera stole him away; and then there was the Homecoming dance last year when two girls made fun of my dress, my hair, my shoes. I felt awful. I felt targeted. I felt like I was living someone else's life. And then I stopped feeling much of anything until you moved to town.

Suddenly I heard a voice yell "Be careful!" and I knew it was the other you at the lab door saying that to the other me when I nearly slipped on the wet ground. That meant it was safe to come out of the pump house and retrieve the brick with the keys. It suddenly occurred to me why my dad made so many sets of keys and why sometimes we couldn't find them. Maybe my parents' weekend jaunts were really time travels. A conversation we had after my dad tried to explain to me the theory of multiple universes replayed itself in my semi-conscious ear.

"Dad," I'd asked, "are you saying there could be an infinite number of worlds?"

"That's the speculation, sweetie, but I'm not saying that. I think there's certainly the possibility of other universes, but like one of the philosophers of the Scientific Revolution, Gottfried Leibniz, I don't think more than one of them exists. Ours."

"But do you mean parallel universes? Could there be another me sitting right here, right now, but in an invisible reality? Do the universes spread out or overlap?"

He laughed then and told me I was too smart for my own good. Then he whispered like he was sharing with only me the most amazing secret, "I know for a fact though, that you can be in two places at once." He winked at me and nodded toward my mother who was busy at her work station, headset on, hands busy, and added, "Your mom's been doing that since she was your age. Just remember that."

I thought he was referring to the fact that she managed to juggle a home and a career and be involved with three civic organizations. But two things about that statement jumped out at me: 'since she was my age' and 'being in two places at once.' It gave me a headache to try to think about that, to imagine my mom at seventeen doing some time jumping and, like me and you, essentially being in two places at once. Of course there was no way for that to happen … unless … unless my parents were traveling back to their pasts.

Out of the blue the urge to vomit overwhelmed me. I tossed the blanket across the next cot and flung myself out the door. I wretched and puked until my sides hurt. I suddenly had a strange question to ask you. I walked slowly to the well, claimed the brick, unlocked the gate and then the door and crept into the lab. The door thumped behind me and I jumped, but I knew the sound was too far away from the other me and the other you who were in the tower by now. I washed my mouth out in the lavatory and gulped down handfuls of water. My heart was doing mini back-flips in anticipation of finding out a certain truth that had been playing around in my head during that long sleep. I walked through the lab and into the hallway, peeked into Mack's room, then knocked on the one across the hall. I waited in the alcove for you to open your door. I didn't give you a chance for a greeting or to tell me if you spied on the other us. I blurted out my question.

"After we crossed the street … in '94 … and we saw Shelly in that car, did we talk to anyone else?"

"Of course. You know that. We went to a dozen places, looking for Megan. We must have talked to a hundred people." Your eyes dilated and tiny flares of light spiked out from your irises. "Well, ten or twelve. You really don't remember?"

"Did we talk to any kids our age?"

"Yeah, why?"

Crap, my head really hurt. "Are you getting a headache too or any other aftereffects? I just threw up a little while ago."

The concern in your eyes was touching. I couldn't have asked for a better friend. "No," you said. "Maybe we should go to a hospital after all. You don't look too good."

I scratched at my face and turned back toward the lab. "No. There's something I have to figure out." My memory flashed on Megan's poor face for an instant and I felt more guilt than anything.

"What?"

"If my parents are time-traveling, too. There are some pieces of memories that I can't quite put together. Something important. Maybe something or someone I saw when we were in '94. Other than Shelly, that is."

You grinned then. "The hot guy. I thought you were obsessing on him the rest of the day and that was why you were such a zombie. You saw him first, but he winked at me."

"What hot guy?"

"You really don't remember? He had a brand-new bike exactly like your old one."

Chapter 13

Something snapped in my head then. Loud. I tingled all over with the realization that not only might my parents be time-traveling to visit their old, or rather young selves, but they might be spying on me in the ultimate parental snooping betrayal ever. They could have told me. They could have taken me along with them. I would have gone eagerly. We could have been a sweet little time-traveling family. Heck, we never took vacations.

"Oh, no," I sighed. I slumped to the floor.

"Really, Laken, where are the car keys? We need to get you to the hospital."

"And tell them what? That I have post time-travel stress disorder?" I attempted a chuckle. It didn't work. I looked up at you, studied the worried look on your face, and shivered. *Mom. I really need to talk to my mom.* All those times she'd tested my blood flashed through my mind. She would have told me if I was anemic or had some disease, wouldn't she? Then the strangest premonition hit me: that I might find my mom under the pump house.

"Sky," I breathed, "stay here." I rose up on wobbly legs. "Just stay here five more minutes." I looked up the hall toward the tower stairs. "Please, please stay here." I turned and went the other way, back through the lab, trusting you would stay put. I held my left hand over the lake and sky pendant and rubbed its smoothness with my thumb and pressed it against my thrumming chest. I took the brick with me because I thought I might need one of the keys.

I walked outside, passed the well, and headed for the pump house. Even with the door wide open and a little more air streaming in, the pump house was no less repulsive. The rain clouds parted for a moment and the sun cast a pool of light across the floor.

I entered and passed from light to dark.

From cool to cold.

And maybe from this world into another.

I shoved two cots out of the way and went straight for the square manhole cover under the thick iron pipes. As I suspected it was a trapdoor, locked, of course. The same key that opened the third-floor door worked on this small access. I set the brick beside my knee. There was less squeaking than I expected as I flipped the panel back on its hinges. The underside displayed a fading symbol, three yellow triangles inside a black circle. The words below the symbol were easily readable.

How stupid was I? Where the heck did bears hibernate except in caves? When my mom and dad discussed the pump house as the perfect place for a long undisturbed sleep they unquestionably meant this manmade cave, the fallout shelter.

I was afraid to peer inside. I might find multiple versions of them—of me—warmly snuggled together in a dark den.

I took a deep breath and braced my hands on the edges. I lowered my head and strained to see into the pitch-black space. It was impossible to make out even the size of it but I assumed it was equal to the pump house, like a basement, but with thicker concrete walls. It smelled vaguely musty with a trace of candle wax. I lifted my head back up before I got dizzy. I thought maybe there'd be a light switch so I reached in and touched around the rough edges. If it was there I couldn't find it. I needed a flashlight or a candle or a phone.

I had a flashlight in the glove box of my car. I had told you to wait five minutes and at least that much time had already passed. I knew I could count on you to keep waiting. I needed to run to the car and back.

I didn't know if the adrenaline helped or hindered my shaky legs, but I got the flashlight rather quickly and doubled back. I shined it down the hole and saw ladder rungs and handholds bolted to the wall. I swiveled around and lowered myself blindly into the opening, caught the first rung and climbed down three steps. With one hand still on the opening of the trapdoor and the other hand swinging the flashlight in every direction I balanced there and took in the strange shelter.

There were four bunk-like beds. Two sat on the floor with two more hanging from chains. A trick of the light made me perceive a slight sway to the one with the blankets. A hand-cranked generator was in the corner along with a toilet. There was a single light bulb in the ceiling with a pull string. A metal shelving unit still held dozens of dusty cans of food, stacked neatly to the edge of each shelf. A waste can next to the shelves held empty cans, garbage which had long ago lost its stink.

Perhaps if we had hibernated down there we would have shivered less in the winter, sweated less in the summer, and not awakened in such bad shape.

Then I had a mind-numbing thought: what if we already did? What if you and I were the ones who ate from those cans, slept on those bunks? What if we did it while our other selves slept on the cots in the pump house above us?

I pulled myself up and out of the shelter, turned the flashlight off and closed the trapdoor. I heard the lock engage. I stood, picked up the flashlight and the brick and dropped them into my bag that lay abandoned on the floor. Bits of grayish skin fell away from the bottom folds as I hefted it up and down to see if the material would still hold so much weight. It did, much better than my mind held the weighty conclusions I was entertaining. I let my new idea swirl around my mind as I left the pump house. I glanced around the garden and wondered if a third me was right that minute somewhere nearby waiting for us to take another trip.

Thankfully, Sky, you were not freaked out that I'd left you alone so long. After all, you'd spent a day and a night there already. Being the best friend that you were, I mean are, you didn't say a word. I found you right where I left you. Almost. You stood at Mack's open door, with Mack in your arms.

"Well, so now he likes you. No more fear face," I said as I set my bag on the floor. "Hello, Mack." I reached my hand out, but he huffed at me and bared his teeth. "Whoa, easy."

"I'll put him back." You moved into his cell and wrenched his wrinkly black fingers from your arms. At ninety pounds Mack was a heavy burden for you and undoubtedly stronger. As well-trained as he was, I didn't completely trust him. I bent down to get the brick out of my bag to use as a weapon if Mack decided to get violent. I'd seen him go ballistic on an intern when he first arrived. That was a moment I'd never forget.

You kept cooing and persuading, your voice lilting with the same sing-song tone my mother used on Mack. It worked. You got him to sit on his bed while you backed out the door. I left the brick in my bag and closed it.

"He got especially agitated when you came back. Should we lock him in?" you asked. You still had your hand on the knob. "Just until we get back from the hospital?"

"I'm not going to the hospital."

"Yes, you are." You turned the bolt and faced me. "I just called your mom from the lab phone. She said they were in the car and would be here in ten minutes."

"They're back already? What a coincidence," I said, sounding like my dad. Then to myself I thought *but there are no coincidences.*

"There are no coincidences," you said, echoing my thoughts and sounding too much like my mom. I blinked away the strangest notion.

"I need to hide my bag. I can't explain to my parents how it got so ratty. And the brick. I need to put that somewhere, too."

"You should have left them both in the pump house."

"Will you put them there for me? I think I'm too weak to do it." The sudden wave of nausea was alarming. Maybe I *was* anemic and needed a blood transfusion. You saw me start to slump.

"What if I stash them in that room?" You obviously didn't want to leave me.

"I've got a better idea. Let's send them in the time machine to where we're going next."

"Where's that?"

"I think we can save Megan if we go back to right after we took the pills." I gritted my teeth against the urge to vomit again. I put my hand on the stone wall for balance and forced a smile. "What do you think?"

"What about that paradox stuff? We already sent her to her grave."

"But if we re-rescue her and take her straight to a hospital in '94 then she won't exist to hibernate and die. And the future hasn't happened yet anyway."

"Hmm, maybe. But we better not see our other selves."

"It'll be all right. Nothing happens, we didn't burst into flame or anything when, just a few minutes ago, I saw you and me get out of my car and come in here. Didn't you watch us walk down this hall?" The nausea passed and I stood a little straighter, dropped my hand from the wall, and breathed easier.

"I didn't look," you said, "but I heard us talking."

"There. See? We *can* be in two places at once."

And maybe there were multiple universes. And maybe I wouldn't be experiencing so many side effects if we time jumped again. I had five more minutes to convince you to go up to the third floor with me again. I didn't want to face my parents yet. Not until I'd made things right.

"In fact," I started slowly smoothing out the lie as I invented it, "we can be in *three* places at once. Because, when I was just in the pump house, I saw us … sleeping … underground." But honestly, Skylar, as soon as the lie was out of my mouth, I knew I could turn it into the truth. "There's a fallout shelter. The key on the brick opens the trapdoor. We're down there right now, Sky, sleeping until any minute now. My parents will be here in five minutes and we'll come dragging around the corner, ready to go to the hospital."

"And Megan? Was she down there?"

"No, um, we must have gotten her to a hospital in '94." I pulled your arm and started toward the tower. "Come on, let's go." If I kept on talking the lie was going to explode on me.

Then the next aftereffect struck me. The center of my vision went black. White hot needles poked my eyes, while icy barbed wire circled my heart. You couldn't have known that and you walked down the hallway unaware of my pain but well aware of my wobbling. I edged my way, fingers on the stone walls, head sideways to depend on my peripheral vision, which was all I had.

"Laken. I don't know. You really seem sick. You can't even walk straight."

"I'll be all right. It's just a little nausea. I told you I puked. I'll be fine as soon as we grab some water and bars on the way up." Actually I thought I was going to die. I so wanted to make it to my next birthday.

Why didn't you experience what I did? What made you immune to time-travel sickness? I was scared senseless. I could not imagine being blind for the rest of my life. The bright lights in the supply room helped some, but I collapsed into the nearest chair and let you fill my bag. You handed me a water and two bars. They definitely did make me feel better. But how was I going to read the controls on the machine?

More than a little panic set in then. I wanted to save Megan. For real. How was I going to do that blind?

"Okay," you said, "let's do it."

We heard the horn honking then. My parents were in the driveway. I must have let the gate latch close and they didn't have their keys. I felt like laughing hysterically, but instead I used the tension to propel me toward the last flight of stairs. You were on my heels.

"You're going to have to pull the switch," I told you as I aimed myself toward the platform. "I don't think I can run and leap like I did before." I climbed onto the platform and curled myself up into a ball around my bag. My conscience was telling me not to run away from my parents, especially not in this condition, but my stubborn will matched my determination.

I looked toward the machine and saw nothing. No controls, no best friend, no chair. Nothing. I moved my gaze to the left and then, faintly out of the corner of my eye, I could make you out standing nervously by the coordinates, a finger in your mouth—that stupid habit of yours.

"Do I change anything?"

I couldn't imagine why you'd need to change anything, but my head was mud so I said, "Make it plus six for the far right elevation. Then hit the lever and run."

I hoped like heck you wouldn't trip. I looked back toward you and of course with that inconvenient blind spot I missed the moment. I heard things though. I heard your squeal. I heard your feet tap the tiles.

And I heard another voice, like an authoritative policeman, you know, like when they shout for some criminal to STOP!

Chapter 14

Time Machine Date: 1994 Again

We fell that second time. Six feet of sudden drop. It was hardly enough time to comprehend what was happening. I landed on my back and then I slid head first a few feet, my bag tumbling from my arms. My breath was knocked out of me.

"You okay?" you screeched from somewhere near my feet.

I couldn't answer right away but I finally filled my lungs, groaned, rolled over and sat up. "That was awful."

"I had half a second to see the ground rushing up at me and brace myself." You rubbed your knees. "I landed hard on my knees and elbows." I *saw* you rub your knees. My eyesight had returned, perfectly normal.

"I guess I shouldn't have told you to add six feet." I looked around then and saw we were on the far side of the hill maybe twenty feet from our previous landing. I chanced rising up and found that my legs supported me, as sturdy and strong as ever. Time-traveling was good for me. There was nothing wrong with my blood; it must have been the hibernation that made me sick. I spotted two fat crows looking down on us from a high branch.

"Oh, crap, Sky. We forgot to get more pills. To hibernate." A heated rush of terror surged through my veins, jetting the horror of our predicament to my heart. The birds emphasized my apprehension with wholehearted cries of their own, flying off toward the woods.

You grabbed at my bag—you hadn't brought yours—and dumped everything out on the grass. We both sorted through the junk in wild panic: four protein bars that went through the long sleep with us, eight new ones, two waters, the frickin' brick, my wallet and money, assorted necessary girl supplies and useless make-up, the LifeStraws, two stupid pens, some tissue and, thankfully, several cases of various sized sleeping pills. We hadn't used them all the first time. The joy, the relief, the happiness I felt to see those pills was slowly replaced with a second spasm of desperation as you opened each case and counted them, mumbling through the math of it. I knew before you finished that we didn't have enough for both of us to make it back. In fact, if I heard your garbled equation correctly, we could either both sleep to 2006 or one of us could wake up around last Christmas while the other lived a different life through the decades.

"Shouldn't be a problem," you smiled. You reached for the lake and sky pendant on my chest and flipped it right side forward.

"Not a problem? What do you mean?"

"Well, if we're going to rescue Megan and take her to a hospital here before the other you and the other me get to her, then they won't need her pills and we should find them where they left them on the cot."

"Impossible," I said, though that had been my idea before we jumped. I was suddenly terribly confused. Obviously. Anyway, the very next moment I started to believe that time was not set in stone and maybe we could do anything we wanted to because it was always the present.

"No, not impossible," you said. "Think about it. It's definitely the afternoon. The sun is over there. It's warmer. We left later in the day so we arrived later. Megan went at night, right? After that party? So she's not even here yet. Time is relative."

Your calculations stunned me. You were so smart and, I hoped, so right. "Are you sure you haven't been interning with my dad?"

"Oh, that reminds me. Let's get to the library. That's where we met that hot guy."

"Wait a minute. What about finding Megan? What about checking the pump house for pills?" I scarcely had my heart back in rhythm and you were thinking about guys. I thought I should remind you that you didn't need to chase after some twentieth century guy when you had a blind date with a college dude next weekend, but I had one more question. "What if the pills aren't there because we really have created a paradox—a contradiction?"

"Yeah, okay. Let's check the pump house."

We stuffed everything back in the bag. We'd left in such a hurry that we not only forgot the most important thing, the pills, but we also forgot the second most important thing, the Mylar blankets. I had some cash left, but not enough for two blankets at fifty bucks each.

We crept slowly toward the pump house. I for one was certain we'd run into a monk or two, but we didn't. I put my hand on the door and you did too, just like the first time, and we shoved. It scraped along the concrete floor, making the same grating sound as the first time which technically was only a few hours ago.

"What did I tell you?" Your voice was a haughty whisper, but you were right. There were three cots set up with our Mylar blankets and some of the protein bars sitting on the middle cot. But no pills.

I snorted. "But this is exactly the way it was. We can't change it. We can't use the blankets or eat the food or anything. If we do, then the first trip will be all screwed up and we wouldn't be here right now. You can't have that kind of … of inconsistency." I didn't say *paradox,* but that's what I was thinking.

"But we *are* here," you argued. "So we didn't screw things up. The other you and the other me are walking around town right now, with the pills in your bag. They'll come back, count out the right amounts, leave them on the cots and go into the monastery for Megan." I sighed and you glared. All I could think of was that you were right about one thing: we *were* here. We hadn't screwed things up yet, but I needed to figure out a different scenario for today. If time travel really did make me smarter, then I could trust the budding seed of an idea that was sprouting in my head. It hinted at the perfect solution.

"Okay," I relented, keeping my thoughts to myself, "what next? Do you want to see the fallout shelter where we'll have to sleep?" I nodded toward the trapdoor and started digging out the brick and keys. "I think I remember seeing woolen blankets on the beds."

"Later. I trust you. Let's go to the library and see if that guy is still there. I can't believe you don't remember seeing him, Laken."

I groaned, stuffed the brick back in the bag, and slung it over my shoulder. I followed you out, half tempted to tell you that your dark roots were even worse now.

"What is it with this old guy? Because that's what he is, you know, in our time he's probably somebody's husband and father."

"We had some kind of a connection. And, and," you gripped my elbow as we found our way to the trail through the woods, "I spent twenty-six years dreaming about him. I *have* to see him again."

I made no comment on that. We angled off at the abandoned car and then I stopped and went back to it. You spent your long siesta dreaming about some nameless guy, but my dreams were fleeting snippets of things. That old car had flashed through my dreams hundreds of times. There was something significant about it, something I'd blocked from my memory. I gave the metal a sharp tap to be sure it actually existed then I turned and caught up to you.

Town was a circus of traffic and people and noise when we got there. I'd been oblivious to everything the first time, but I took it all in with an eye out for the grown-up Shelly Ayers. She rather freaked me out before.

"There he is," you gushed. Yeah, that's right, I said gushed. You sounded like a lovesick Juliet—played by a bad actress—sorry. "He's just coming out of the library. Come on." Your excited smile was probably visible from the space shuttle.

I hung back and watched the reunion. You'd clearly made an impression on him too. He motioned for you to sit with him on the bench in front of the library sign and you completely forgot about me. I leaned against the nearest tree and let my bag rest on a root. He was cute all right, and he had two dimples and very dark hair, but I had no clue as to why you thought he looked like my dad. Unless it was his eyes. Shocks of that dark hair kept covering them and he'd either flick his head or run his hand through the strands.

Your conversation was inane. Not in a frivolous, ridiculous sort of way, but rather in a scientific, boring, oh-you-like-animals-too sort of way. Still, it was sweet and the guy was definitely hot even if there was no future in your relationship. Well, that's what I thought then, but actually, Skylar, you *have* to get to know him better. That's vital to our futures.

After half an hour I shortened the distance between us and gave you a gentle reminder that we needed to go. "Come on, Sky, we need to get a lot of food."

You jumped up as if you were surprised that I was still around.

"Laken, remember C.J.? He was just telling me he got a scholarship to U of M."

"Congratulations." I stuck my hand out like an idiot and he stood up and shook it.

"Thanks."

Reluctantly I drew my hand back, but the heat of his fingers remained. An inner voice said, *'He's not interested in you. He likes Skylar.'* But inside, a little warm glow spread. He had kind eyes. How could I not be attracted to him?

"He was just telling me how he won that mountain bike."

That fact sent shivers up my spine. My dad had been one of five kids to win a bike—the very bike I still used—way back when he was a kid. What if this C.J. knew my dad?

"Cool." I grasped at the lake and sky pendant and glanced around half expecting to see my dad somewhere.

"Nice locket," he said.

I babbled breathlessly about why we bought it together, how it represented our friendship, and that it was my turn to wear it for the next twenty-six years. You bumped your shoulder against mine to shut me up and gave a fake laugh.

"Okay, then," you said. "We really have to go. Maybe we'll run into you again."

"Sure. Hey, how about tonight?" He tucked his hands in his pockets and let that gorgeous hair fall over his eyes.

I felt like a third wheel or whatever they call that awkward extra person when two people of the opposite sex only have eyes for each other. I mumbled a *'see ya'* and headed toward the drug store before you could include me in your date with him or ask if he had a friend for me.

I went through the automatic doors and headed for the snack food aisle. I was holding a carton of body-building high protein bars when you caught up to me.

"What were you thinking?" I said. "You can't make a date here."

We went down the make-up aisle sounding like two ordinary teenagers having an argument, me saying you couldn't see that guy tonight and you saying it would all work out … what was meant to be, would be … there were no coincidences … blah, blah, blah … you were going to meet him at six o'clock no matter what I said. I stopped listening when I caught a glimpse of a bearded man turning quickly down the next aisle.

"Fine," I said. "Just don't meet him at the Big Boy or there'll be a paradox for sure."

"I'm not stupid. We're meeting at that restaurant by the river. But there's one thing," you said, turning on the charm. "Can I wear the pendant?"

I put my hand on the smooth glass and that germ of an idea that had sprouted in my head finished its blossoming. My puny anger dissipated and I returned your stare with a look of blinding innocence and batted my naked eyelashes at you. "Of course."

Chapter 15

W e bought mostly junk food and ate as much as we could before heading to the dollar store. We kept a good lookout for our other selves, at least I did, but luckily we never saw ourselves. With two of my last ten dollars I bought a couple of cheap plastic clocks. They probably wouldn't last a week, but we only needed them for a few hours. For my plan to work timing needed to look critical.

We decided to wait down by the river. There were only the rocks to sit on—it was going to be a lot nicer in twenty years when the city would add a walkway, benches, and picnic tables—but we enjoyed the warm afternoon anyway and I listened to you repeat every silly word that passed between C.J. and you. Three times. Then we forced ourselves to eat more. You kept looking up the path toward the restaurant where you were going to meet this man of your dreams. You checked your clock and sighed a dozen times. I could have gagged, Sky.

"Are you sure you don't mind waiting out here a couple of hours, Laken?"

"Of course not. What are best friends for?"

Then you got quiet for a while before you asked me a second, a third, and a fourth time the same question. Every time I insisted it was no big deal, not to worry, I understood, blah, blah, blah.

During those quiet moments I reviewed my plan in my head. You would go in the restaurant at six and instead of waiting here as I promised umpteen times, I'd run back to the pump house, lock myself in the fallout shelter, take all the pills I had, and hibernate as long as possible. I wouldn't make it to April, but I'd have the brick with me and I could let myself in the lab. I could use the machine to go forward, pack up plenty of supplies and pills, and jump back here. I'd be right here when your date ended and you'd never know I left. That was my plan. I was a genius. What could go wrong?

At five minutes to six I reminded you, "If we're going to catch Megan as soon as she lands we need to be back to the lab, I mean monastery, before the other you and the other me get there. You have to watch the time while you're with this guy, this C.J., so keep the clock on the table or in your lap." I dug in my bag for the money. Our last eight dollars. "Here, take this. In case he's not paying."

It must have been the look on my face that gave away my opinion of this whole setup because you took the money and stroked the pendant, talking to it instead of to me: "Lake and Sky. Sky and Laken. We are best friends for a reason. There are no coincidences." Then you looked me in the eye and said, "See ya soon."

I had to smile back at you then even though I was slightly irritated that you were abandoning me for this stranger. Sure, it was only for a couple of hours, but it would be years for me. And I was doing this, risking who knew what new side effects, just so I could get you back to 2020. Because, truthfully, I didn't think we could re-rescue Megan. There was no way we could change what we already did. I'd seen death on Megan's face and if there's one thing I've learned it's that there's nothing you can do then but move on.

So ... I did it. I left you in '94. Sorry, sorry, sorry. I did not intend to take the sleep agent by myself the second time we went back in time. I'm sorry about that. There were other things I didn't mean to do that day.

Like leave you alone with the cutest boy I'd ever met.

Or steal your share of the sleep agents you'd need to jump through time.

Or bolt the door from the inside so you couldn't search the pump house for any extra pills.

You could stomp on that door for two and a half decades, but then you'd be old and I'd still be young. You'd have to find another safe place to wait for my return or grow up in that other generation.

Honestly, I was sorry. I didn't mean to leave you forever. That was not my intention. You have to believe that. I intended to come back for you so we could figure out together where to hibernate and how many milliliters or milligrams to take. You knew better than I did how to calculate that stuff. Numbers—the one little failing of that big brain of mine.

I intended to hibernate—suffer the aftereffects—collect some more pills and send myself back for you. I did it for your sake. Honest. But it didn't work out that way and that's how the whole chronology of my life—and yours—got all mixed up.

So anyway, I raced back through the woods, past the junked car, and quietly crept into the pump house and closed the door. I left everything undisturbed, which was tricky in the late afternoon gloom, but I could see like a cat. I didn't trip over the cots or have any trouble unlocking the fallout shelter. I tossed the brick in to where I thought the closest bunk bed was, heard it clunk, and then I dropped my bag straight down. There was no turning back then. I stuck my foot in and found the ladder. Ten cautious steps later I reached the bottom and almost tripped on my bag. I walked forward with my arms raised, feeling for that ceiling light string and imagining a dozen other nightmarish things that could be hanging there instead. When my left hand felt it, I pulled gently and the bulb dimly illuminated the room.

There. I'd done it. Step one: Sneak away from you. Check. Step two: Get into the hibernation room. Check.

I cranked up the generator with what little time-traveling strength I could muster and the light shined more brightly. Good to know that was all it took. I shook out the blankets and tested the mattresses. My bag was going to stay on the lower bunk on the wall by the toilet and I was going to nap on the one above it. I climbed up and tested the distance to the ceiling light string. I'd be able to turn the light off after I took the pills and when I woke up I could swing my arm out and find it again.

I checked my cheap little clock and tried to estimate how much longer before the other me and the other you would return from town. I went up the ladder and pulled the trapdoor closed, heard it latch and then tried to open it again. From this side I didn't need the key. That was a relief since it would be terribly cumbersome to hold the key upwards from the heavy brick and not knock myself in the nose.

I climbed back down and cave the generator enough cranking to hold a charge for a while. Then I heard a scraping above my head. I froze. I figured I didn't have to turn out the light. The other me and the other you weren't going to notice. They would count pills and then go looking in the monastery for Megan.

I got goose bumps listening to our voices above. Muffled. I couldn't make out the words, but I remembered the conversation: you had called Shelly Ayers a sociopath; you had said I was zoning out; I had explained my brilliant reasoning why Megan had to be in the monastery—chalk one up for Laken Mitchell—and then we had laughed about monks and monkeys.

The voices stopped. When I was sure they—we—had gone to the monastery I was extremely tempted to sneak up and follow behind them—us—and watch through the cracks, but I restrained myself. The minutes dragged for me as I pictured us trespassing into the monastery and bringing Megan back. When I thought enough time had passed, I turned my light off and sat there straining to hear us return.

The door scraped. We were back and making those last-minute preparations. I heard the thump of a foot stepping hard on the trapdoor. Why was that? Then I remembered; it must have been you retrieving the pills that rolled toward the pipes when Megan fell onto her cot.

I breathed slowly. I was starting to shiver. The warm June night above didn't visit this cellar. In the blackness I began to imagine this as my coffin and the thought was enough to get me breathing faster. The sounds above stopped. I ached to turn on the light. Five more minutes snailed by like twenty. I counted to a thousand and pulled the string.

It was time to take my hibernation pills and wrap up warmly, but there was no way I was going to fall asleep in the dark. I took a colossal paradox-provoking chance and went back up top.

The light from my shelter streamed out from the edges of the opening as my head poked through. Three steadily breathing sleepers were a few minutes into their comas, and completely unaware of me, their subterranean intruder. I pushed the door all the way over and came up. My phone was glowing on the floor by the other me. I stepped over Megan and picked it up. I stared at my sleeping other self and softly called my name, "Laa-ken."

No movement. The other me was out for the century.

For a moment I considered sleeping on the fourth cot which was wedged in tightly to secure the door. My weight would add to its safety value, but I had a plan already and since I was on my own, I wanted to stick to it. Well, that wasn't the only reason. I pictured you finding your way through the woods, if not tonight, then tomorrow, if I didn't make it back according to my plan. The fact that you hadn't shown up yet was definitely in my favor. It gave me the confidence that my plan would work. Of course, it could be that you were falling in love and not looking at the clock.

Unquestionably both of us were suffering from paradox fever or hibernation illness. Your obsession with this stranger was obvious evidence of that. Funny how the time traveling and hibernation affected us so differently.

I slipped back down into my cave, took all the pills, drank the water, turned off the ceiling light and by the flashlight app on my phone I bundled myself up as tightly as I could.

Once more I fell asleep to the waning glow of my phone.

My last thoughts were:

Step one, sneak away from you. Check.

Step two, get into the hibernation room. Check.

Step three, take the pills. Check.

Step four, wake up.

Wake up.

Chapter 16

Time Machine Date: 2019 and 2020

W ake up.

Pitch black darkness gave way to gray-black blindness when I opened my eyes on what I later learned was the morning of Friday, December 20, 2019. I knew exactly where I was since I had been dreaming of this burial chamber for years.

Opening my eyes was far easier that time than after my first hibernation. I blinked without difficulty. There was no buildup of crusty gunk around my eyes or nose. My mouth was dry like before but nowhere near as bad. I stretched and groaned and tested every muscle. I revived like I did on a normal Saturday morning when I could wake up unhurried.

I threw my arm outward and caught the ceiling light string on the first try. The light bulb gave off all of maybe ten watts, but that was enough to get myself off the top bunk without falling in a heap. I yawned and stretched some more and gave the generator five cranks, all I could manage. The light brightened and I stood there feeling pretty good. I rubbed at my arms expecting to see the zombie-effect, but there was minimal skin flaking. Obviously it was better to hibernate in a constant, cool environment.

My bag sat undisturbed on the lower bunk. I put the brick in it and picked it up. The brick broke through the bottom, thwacked the edge of the bunk and landed on my foot. Apparently, the cooler temperatures hadn't kept it from rotting for a second quarter-century. I choked on the yelp that erupted from my throat. I pushed the bag underneath the bed, out of sight, collected the brick and my phone and left the light to burn for however long that took.

Pushing the trapdoor up was exciting. I didn't know then what time of day it was or how long I'd slept. I set the brick and my useless phone on the floor and hoisted myself through the opening. The stillness was broken by a mouse that ran up the beam and disappeared. The trapdoor slammed shut unexpectedly and I jumped forward, crushing my phone. In the back of my mind I knew that had to happen. I kicked it across the floor where the other me would find it in about three and a half months.

"Laa-ken. Mee-gan. Skyy-lar." My voice sang out, not scratchy or tinny or the slightest bit out of tune. Of course, the three sleeping beauties didn't appreciate my morning song to them. Not one of them moved. I stepped next to Megan and said a little prayer for her. I hoped her dreams were life enough for her. I stared at you, Skylar, the first you that is, and hoped I was doing the right thing for you. I moved over to my body and tucked the blanket a little tighter around the edges. Nobody seemed to be shivering. Actually they looked dead, but I knew they weren't.

The fourth cot barred the door. I wondered how I was going to get out and still keep the door barred. But that was one thing I'd put on the worry list for later. Time travel made me smarter, right? I'd figure it out.

I left vague footprints in the hardened snow between the pump house and the gate, but since it was still snowing they'd be

113

covered soon. I was shivering from the freezing winter weather, but that was a low priority when I saw car tracks and then king-size footprints. John, the intern, had walked here from the college campus and was inside working. I unlocked the gate and walked down the slope expecting to see maybe my dad's car or mine, but it looked like I'd be alone with John. Not a pleasant thought.

John had left the door unlocked. I entered, grabbed the red hooded zip sweater my mom kept on a hook by the door and slipped it on. I flipped the hood up over my hasn't-been-washed-in-years hair, and entered the lab as nonchalantly as possible.

I carried the brick in my right hand and swirled the keys around letting the annoying jangle announce my presence. John was at one of the computers. He jerked his head up and his facial expression changed from his usual leer to surprise when he saw me.

"What the hell happened to you?"

"Sleep over," I said. More like sleep under.

"Must have been one hell of a party. I thought you had school today. Last day before Christmas break."

That's when I knew exactly what day it was. I smirked to myself. My parents were off on a "shopping" holiday and I was in school that very moment enduring the first of several lame holiday parties. There'd be candy canes, piñatas, too much pizza, and a quiz in Schemanski's class which, if you remember, you would outscore me on by two points.

"I thought I'd skip," I said, trying to think of a not-too-obvious way to avoid walking right by him to head for the stairs, "and clean the cages or take inventory on the second floor."

"You shouldn't skip school. You don't want to turn into one of *those* girls, do you?"

He looked me up and down and my cheeks flushed hot. I imagined strips of skin falling off my face like before. We were a good twenty-five feet apart, close enough for me to see the Band-Aid around the finger he was tapping on a brick similar to mine and close enough for him to notice how wretched I looked.

"I need to use the restroom." I turned and raced away, faster than you'd think, considering my recovery time before. Come to think of it, I didn't recover before. I time jumped and that cured my nausea, headache, blindness, and overall hibernation sickness. Maybe I'd built up an immunity to the aftereffects.

I checked myself in the mirror and, aside from the dye job on my hair sporting about two inches of lighter roots, I was fairly presentable. I considered a quick shower, but the idea of getting naked with John in the building made my skin crawl. I settled for washing my face and hands really well. After all I was only going to be here a few minutes. I could jump back to '94 as soon as I stuffed my pockets with capsules of sleep agent, some fresh protein bars, water, and money. My brain was working at time-travel velocity. I couldn't wait to see you, Sky, and challenge you to some I.Q. quizzes. Math even.

The only problem I could see was how to sneak the capsules out of the drawer where John was working. If I had to wait all day, I guess I could. He was bound to take a bathroom break sooner or later. In the meantime, I'd figure out how many pills I'd need.

I put the hood back up and zipped the sweater. I boldly walked back through the lab and stopped at the mice cages. They were clean. John was actually a pretty efficient intern and I wondered why he was going to leave at Christmas without even giving my parents any notice instead of continuing to work here next semester. Not that it mattered. I was glad he was going to quit early since it meant that I would get to help with the pills and learn enough to successfully time jump and hibernate back. If he only knew …

I jangled the keys again. "I'm going to do some inventory upstairs. See ya later."

He grunted.

I walked down the cell hallway, climbed the stairs, and entered the supply area. My taking inventory was going to be all about eating and drinking. I was starving. I set the brick on the trunk of money.

That's when I got the worst surprise of my life. John, like a ninja, had followed me. He yanked my hood back and blurted out a nasty curse when he saw my black hair.

"Keep your hands off me," I screeched at him, my heart in my throat.

"What'd you do to your hair?"

"None of your business."

"Maybe it is. Because maybe you owe me for covering for you."

"What are you talking about?" I felt the burn start in my feet and rise. I glanced to where I'd set the brick.

"The police have interviewed me more than once. I never told them about your friend, the one you brought here. The one who left her shoes in Mack's room." The muscles around his mouth quivered as he attempted to fool me with a smile. "You owe me. I know you did something to that girl. Helped her run away, maybe?"

He reached his hand out.

"Don't touch me!"

He moved his hand to point. "Her shoes are over there. Did you know there was blood on them? Did you do something else to her, Laken?"

I couldn't believe how threatening his tone was. This jerk had obviously been waiting and waiting to get me alone.

Maybe he wanted money. He couldn't know what was inside of the trunk. I could bribe him to leave me alone.

I glanced over to where he indicated and recognized the bright green sneakers that Megan had been wearing that night. Who could forget them?

John waved his phone in front of my face, touched the screen, and brought up a picture of me and Megan, our backsides walking away from him. Okay, so he had proof I knew her and that she'd been at the lab the night she disappeared.

John was quick. He grabbed me, pushed me down, and violently tore at the clothes under the red sweater.

His vile language was peppered with threats that he'd get what he wanted and not to fight him or I'd go to jail.

I fought. I swear my brain was fighting as hard as my weakened muscles, but I would never have a chance against the strength of a twenty-one-year-old male intent on harming a weakened time-traveling idiot. Unless, my brain told me like a cheering spectator, unless I smashed his reptilian skull with the lock block, the lab slab, the frickin' brick.

Anybody who did what I did could and probably would kill someone. Accidentally … or not so accidentally.

What happened next was pure panicked instinct. He tried to kiss my neck and face in the worst possible way, clawing at me, biting, growling, pushing my head hard against the floor. I used one hand to shove his face away, pounding on him with the other. I thrashed my legs, trying to get my knee into his groin.

117

His grunts and groans quickened, my screams faltered. I kicked at the trunk and the brick slipped off. There was no murderous intent when I stopped pounding him to reach for the only weapon around. My determination was only to get him to stop.

I must have swung the brick too hard.

And too many times.

One minute he was alive and the next … not so much.

I didn't know how relief and torment could share a moment so completely. The silence and stillness were ghostly.

I wormed my way out from under his still body while silent tears fled down my cheeks.

What had I done?

I kicked at his feet. "Wake up. Wake up."

He didn't move. I checked his pulse. His heart still beat.

That wasn't the first, or even the second near-death that I had to separate from my conscious thought and lock away in a mental casket. I could feel myself getting older, growing up too fast, like the hibernation was catching up to me. My heart was pounding way too fast.

I had to think. I needed a plan.

I held John's head while more tears blinded me. If I lost control, I knew I'd scream incessantly.

The blood was easy to clean up. Getting him up the stairs and onto the platform … big problem. I couldn't do it by myself. I seriously considered waking up my other self and the other you to help me, but since I didn't have that particular memory, I couldn't chance a paradox.

Megan's sleeping self, on the other hand, was a feasible alternative. My brain was firing fast then and I remembered the spray bottle of Hiber-wake next to all the sleep agent pills. I also remembered Megan's cryptic message before she died: '*send the beast to hell.'* Remember, Sky? It made perfect sense: in her timeline I'd already used her to help me. I must have told her what a beast John was and that he'd tried to rape me. And that we had to send him to hell. That was what I intended to do—hell being the now snow-covered hill beyond the pump house. Sorry, John.

I gathered every personal thing John had brought to the lab: a picture, his jacket, several books, a brown bag lunch and six Cokes. My heart was threatening to burst out of my chest before I made it to the third floor. I set his stuff on the platform and hurried back down. I gathered other evidence: Megan's shoes. They were going to get a funeral, too.

It was so wrong. I knew it was wrong. But I couldn't help myself, Sky. Besides, I had an alibi. I was at school eating pizza and Christmas cookies—with you!

I wasted ten minutes trying to figure out how many pills of which size to give Megan afterward to make her sleep for a hundred eight days. I knew I got it right. I stuffed them in the pocket of the red hooded sweater and zipped the sweater up over my ripped shirt.

The snow was silently drifting down. I hurried through it and re-entered the pump house.

Megan woke up after one whiff of whatever was in that spray bottle. I hustled her out of the pump house before she could see there were two of me. Then I was super careful leading her through the snow. I didn't want her loose flesh to fall off and leave a trail of blood and skin in the stark whiteness. She was barefoot and the toe prints she left were disturbing. Not to mention the fact that I'd already seen her die about three months from then. Maybe that was going to be my fault for waking her up now.

I had no idea what the drugs, the sleep agent, and the Hiber-wake spray together would do to her mental state, but I was already confident that this plan was destined to succeed. I repeated over and over that she had a mission to *'send the beast to hell.'*

Megan nodded and sleep-walked behind me like the zombie she was though there was no leg-dragging or arm-swinging.

Mack heard us as we passed and began to make a pant-hoot sound followed by a very distinctive 'wraaa' call which added to the 'beast' fear that I'd recited to Megan.

When we got to the second floor and she saw John lying so still she didn't require any coaxing to help me get him to the 'hospital' on the third floor.

It was amazing how helpful she was in her much-altered state.

We dragged him up—super hard for the two us—and laid him on the platform with his things. Megan reached for her shoes that were there, but I gently directed her into the chair and told her to close her eyes. I tapped the controls, the coordinates bright on the screen, and sent John and all trace of him a safe ten feet under the hill beyond the pump house, year 2035. The machine made its customary roar, a sort of shockwave or sonic clap that completed the transaction. I was ready to reassure Megan, but she hadn't flinched.

"One more thing, Megan, just to be safe."

She opened her eyes. "What? Oh, I forgot your name."

"It's Laken. Laken Mitchell." But I'm going to have to change it, I thought.

"What thing? What one more thing?" She was woozy and I wondered which hibernation sickness was going to present itself next.

"Special pills, Megan. Just for you. Come on."

120

That motivated her. I checked outside for cars before we walked in our snow prints back to the pump house. She hadn't complained about being barefoot. She was still in a lethargic stupor. You'd say she was zoned out.

I told her the party had morphed into a sleep-over. "Here," I said as we entered the pump house. She held her hand out for the pills and popped them one by one. "This is what you do, Megan, I'm going back outside to stand watch and you're going to set this cot up to bar the door. Then wrap yourself in that blanket and … have a nice trip."

And that was that. I tested the door a minute later and she had done it; she'd barred the door and no one, no cops even, would open it until you, that first you, would wake up.

The snow was falling harder then and our footprints would be obscured in half an hour. I locked the gate and then the door, turned off the lights, gathered all the supplies I'd already thought of and started for the third floor.

That's when I heard the car engine.

That's when I hurried too fast.

That's when the machine was too warm, too recently used, to let me input the date or coordinates I wanted. There was no going back to 1994. The only dates it would accept were yesterday or April 5th. How strange was that? I chose April 5th, the day after we first time-traveled, prayed that the default coordinates wouldn't bury me, and sprang for the white platform.

Jumping back to 1994 had been virtually instantaneous, but going forward, traveling to the future, was incredibly slow, not to mention painful.

I crossed the room in a second and a half, twisted myself mid-air and landed sitting upright on the platform facing the controls and the open door. The open door. Crap. I'd left the brick holding it ajar. I had maybe one second left to jump off the machine and start over, but the risk of only parts of me getting sent to the future kept all of me stuck on the white plastic.

There was a frozen moment when I knew I was in two places at once, or maybe I was in the future and the past all at once. I don't think my heart took a second beat. Every fiber, every muscle was paralyzed. I couldn't blink or even move my eyes right or left. A hundred billion neurons screamed their pain, but I couldn't move. Ninety thousand miles of sensations all fired at once and it wasn't good.

With no power to scream I had to endure, wide-eyed and fixed, the unbelievably long trip. There was a strobe light effect to what I could see, as if I were being made to reflect on a time lapsed set of photos that revealed the same boring view of the door and the controls, but with infinitesimal changes in the light. Then enormous changes.

I caught a startling moment of my father standing there, lights on, lights off.

Then it was an eternity of the mostly graying snapshot of the door, now closed, and the controls. I wanted to scream. If only I could scream. My nervous system was on overload.

Then the boring picture changed for an instant and I saw a stranger. The entire awful trip continued like that: me staring like a statue at a static scene that only rarely changed and then only for an instant. It seemed like years between getting a quick look at something new like my mom by herself, then my mom and my dad together, then Mack in my dad's arms. And then what seemed like years of the same still room, the present—the long moment I was in—shrouded in formless clouds and vacant depths. Inwardly I shuddered at the thought of plunging into nothingness.

Who would want to travel into the future that way? No wonder poor Mack was so different after he jumped forward.

There were instances when what I saw was right in front of me. Inches away. I'd hit a red hot wall of heat and noise and I knew that was when someone else was getting in the machine and taking an immediate trip to the past.

I saw for the briefest of moments myself, an excited grin frozen on my face, mid-leap, and I knew that in that instant I was sitting next to the original you and everything was just beginning for the 'past' me on April 4th. The trip was just about to end for the 'present' me and the machine was a few painful moments away from spitting me out on April 5th.

My heart finished the single beat it started a hundred nineteen days before and continued thumping, fast at first, then it slowed. The pain was over. I blinked. I was still on the platform in one piece. I hadn't been spewed out on the hill beyond the pump house. The machine made a deafening crack, like a sonic boom. My trip was officially over.

At that precise moment, with the certainty that some things were preordained and inescapable, I sensed I would never see you again.

I slipped to the floor and lay my head on the cool tile and kept still until the dreadful premonition faded.

I lifted my head and when I was sure I wasn't going to have any sudden aftereffects, I checked my pockets and made certain I had enough pills and enough money to go back to '94. I was exhausted, but I wasn't going to surrender to a hopeless premonition. I had to go immediately.

I rose and checked the control screen. It was blinking red and green error messages. The last loud noise produced by that very important machine was nothing less than its failure to reboot. I tried every computer trick I knew including pulling the plug. The backup batteries kept the lights flashing and I gave up.

The thing about time-traveling to the future was that it magnified my past. The pain wasn't merely a hell I endured, it clarified every moment of my life, the good and the bad.

The error message of my life was that I had deceived my parents and betrayed their trust and, most awfully, become a murderer. And now I'd apparently broken the machine. I needed to tell them about that, and about the missing girls, and the really bad stuff, and that I'd left you in the last century.

I felt hopeful at that moment despite the grief and guilt and despite the non-functioning machine. Who else would understand the art of time travel and hibernation, and its coincidences, better than Conner and Emily Mitchell?

I didn't care if they grounded me for a year or turned me over to the police, I needed to come clean about everything if there was the slightest chance to rescue you, Sky.

Chapter 17

My car was sitting where I'd parked it a mere day ago, speckled with raindrops from the April showers, the ignition key under the mat, our bathing suit purchases in the back seat along with those easily forgotten job application forms. But I had no frickin' brick. Most likely my dad had found it and taken it home. I could imagine him stroking his beard and wondering how he had misplaced it yet again. I'd left it in the past and for that reason I couldn't open the gate and drive home.

Not that I was going to drive home. No way. I wasn't leaving until that machine got fixed and I could go back for you. If my parents had to come to the lab to open the gate for me, they'd come inside and find me in this nasty physical state. I probably wouldn't be able to convince my dad, once he repaired the time machine, to let me travel back, but not getting permission hadn't stopped me before.

Of course nothing ever turns out in my life the way I plan. I called my mom's cell and she went crazy on me, yelling and crying. She told me where to find a spare gate key and insisted that I drive home immediately. She'd just had a call from your parents and then the police. She seemed much more upset to have spoken with your mother than with the detective assigned to search for you. Sorry to say, Skylar, you were now another of our town's missing girls. I'd better get home, mom warned, before my father did. I wondered where he would have gone on a Sunday afternoon. I pondered that the whole drive home.

"Ah! You found my red sweater," my mother exclaimed when I walked in the door. That wasn't the reaction I expected.

"You'd better go shower and change. You're a mess." Then she threw her arms around me and started balling. Also not what I expected.

"Where's dad?" I said as soon as she let go of me. She was still gulping those shuddering breaths.

"Out." She eyed the bulging pockets on my sweater and I finally got the reaction I anticipated.

"Laken Marie Mitchell! Empty those pockets!"

I spilled sleep agent pills and wads of cash onto the kitchen table. My mom gasped and threw a hand over her mouth. She paced from the table to the stove and back. I'd never seen her so angry, yet so sad. She grated her teeth and repeated, "There are no coincidences. There are no coincidences." Then she grabbed me again, burst out with more hysterical sobs, and squeezed me nearly to death.

"Mom. Mom."

"We thought we'd lost you, Laken. I've been up all night." She slumped into a kitchen chair and I sat down, too. "We got home. You were gone. We found your car at the lab, but no trace of you." She paused and stared right through me. "And no bodies in the pump house."

My chest tightened to that breathless point of compression. I saw something in my mother's face I'd never seen before. The sudden luster in her red-rimmed eyes and the feverish blush to her cheeks abandoned her for a second and I saw the look that would be on your face the moment you realize you were stuck in 1994—if I didn't go back.

"Mom? Please don't have a heart attack. I'm fine." I opened my mouth again to say that I lost you, but it came out, "And Sky's fine." Her left eyebrow went up at that. "And of course there are no bodies in the pump house." Both brows begged to differ with me then. She could always tell when I was hiding the truth.

The basement door opened then and my dad flew into the kitchen. He lifted me in a bear hug and laughed out words that didn't fit. "You made it. You did it. Oh, honey, I'm so relieved. I didn't know where you'd end up."

He let me drop back into my chair and he pulled out another and sat heavily, all of us then in our usual spots for dinner, with nothing set on the table except bills and pills.

My dad lost his jubilation in an instant and turned quite serious. He clenched his lips together so tightly that they disappeared behind the beard and mustache. I braced myself for the worst.

"All right, young lady, we have a big mess to clean up. We know a little about the girls you've been helping this past year. We know all about the first and the last ones, Shelly Ayers and Megan Hodges. Now, who was second? What happened?"

So they *had* been spying on me, but why did they only know about Shelly and Megan? Those were the only two that you knew about. And I knew you hadn't tattled.

"We're waiting, Laken." My father's impatience was new to me.

My mom put her hand over mine and said, "Honey, Skylar's parents are not going to stop until they, their lawyers, the police, the media, everybody gets to the bottom of this and they bring Sky home. We have to cover it all up. And we have to be quick."

"So you knew I was using the time machine?"

There was a fairly crowded silence and then, "We knew. We allowed it. We're all in this together."

I wanted to let my head sink into my hands and cry in relief. I'd hated all the sneaking around, the middle of the night

127

trespasses, and most of all the lying. I kept my head up and trusted my parents with the truth, the whole truth. Almost.

"Shelly Ayers was first. I hated her. She humiliated me in middle school." I glanced at my dad. He wouldn't understand since it was a girl thing so I skipped ahead. "Anyway, even though she totally embarrassed me a long time ago I helped her escape her really bad home life and I got so much satisfaction from sending her to the past that I started looking for other girls who needed to disappear."

Then I told them all about number two, Erica Wills.

Erica was a gossip, a bitch, a jerk, and probably the sleaziest girl in our class. But she was beautiful and popular. I never understood why she was so well liked even though people always got into fights with her. After she disappeared nobody but me could think of anything bad to say about her and I was keeping my mouth shut.

Erica and Melissa were the two girls who made fun of me at the Homecoming dance my sophomore year.

"Hey, Pond," Erica said, trying to be cute and funny. "Where did you get that dress?"

Another girl standing by, a snarky freshman named Melissa, saw her chance to rise in the ranks and offered a response before I could, "She must shop at the Salvation Army. It was all the rage in the seventies." Her laugh was like a virus and everyone within earshot caught it and laughed along.

My date, probably the nicest if not the dorkiest boy in our school, laughed too. I forgave him later when he swore to heaven and back that he'd never heard of the Salvation Army and thought they were complimenting me since I looked so beautiful. Yeah, Skylar, he said beautiful.

But after some awkward dancing Erica swung by our table and commented on my shoes, wondering how anyone with feet as big as mine could find grandma-heels in size twelve. I was tongue-tied. I'd worn low heels so I wouldn't be taller than my date. Did my feet look big? I pretended to have a coughing fit and headed to the restroom.

It wasn't over though. I was the flavor of the night for Erica. Melissa, too. She was already in the restroom giggling with four other ninth grade girls who were wearing enough make-up to supply all the street-walkers in Detroit. I walked in, saw her, and turned around to head out, but Erica was right behind me, surrounded by an entourage of equally mean girls.

"Hey, swamp, let's fix your hair for you."

There was no fighting off nine pairs of manicured hands. They pushed me to the filthy restroom floor where I sat beneath their flying fingers which scratched at my scalp and pulled at my hair.

After their make-over I looked like a scarecrow. I texted my date to meet me in the parking lot. He took me home without a word.

I managed to stay off their radar after that. I got my license, had the 'experience' with Shelly Ayers, sending her back to '63, and I was confident about not getting caught. I ran into Erica Wills by herself and she acted all friendly and actually apologized for her bad behavior before asking me to lend her ten dollars. I gave her two fives. An idea popped into my head. I told her I was having a party and did she want to come and bring her cute friends? I knew she was using me, but she didn't know that I was using her. There was always that chance that some of her popularity could rub off on me. Or, I could get a chance, on my own turf, to get even. I was open to either way things might go.

129

Her friends were pretty mad when they found out my parents didn't keep any liquor in the house. Somebody arrived with a case of beer then and I thought that meant their anger would subside. Wrong. They trashed the place.

Erica passed out on my bed. Eventually her friends left, even the one who gave her a ride over, so I helped her into my car. The brick was on the passenger's side floor because I'd been too lazy to put it back in the house after the last time I'd used it. Erica kept kicking her foot on it and making fun of people who were so stupid they couldn't remember where they put their keys so they had to tie them to a brick. Ha, ha, ha.

It was one in the morning and I had a golden opportunity for revenge. I couldn't help myself. I took her to the lab. She was not too drunk to walk up to the third floor, but she was definitely too out of it to realize that my telling her to lie down on the 'massage table' was not going to end well for her.

I chose that day's date and some random coordinates close to what was already on the screen. What did I care?

Poof, the bitch was gone. And nobody was going to think anything other than that she ran away from home.

I locked up and stepped outside. The dark monastery in the middle of the woods was creepy enough after midnight, but before I could open the car door I heard far off shrieks, like the sound a rabbit makes when a bobcat pounces. The screams were faint at first, then frantic. And human. I grabbed the flashlight from the car, pushed the gate all the way open and ran for the path to town. Between the ghastly moonlight and the fairly strong beam in my hand I followed the trail to the rusty car. The cries were growing less frequent.

"Help me."

Erica was impaled on the bumper of the old vehicle. A part of her left leg was buried in the ground along with her left arm up to her elbow. She looked like someone rising out of bed, but sinking down at the same time. Blood dripped into the dirt.

I choked back bile to keep my hysteria at bay. "Shh, I'll get you out. Stop screaming."

I searched around for something to dig with and used a couple of sticks to free her leg and arm from the ground. I pulled on her to help her stand and the shriek that pierced the night was unearthly. A rusty shard of metal broke off and more blood gushed.

"I'm so sorry. I'm so, so sorry." I really was. She didn't deserve what was happening to her, not for being mean to me, and not for being a bully, or anything. But what could I do? She'd seen the time machine. Even drunk she had to realize she traveled from the lab into the forest, into the ground actually, by incomprehensible means.

I tore off my shirt and tied it around her, hoping to stem the awful flow of blood. I needed her to walk back. We got halfway back before she dropped to her knees. She'd soaked through my shirt and neither of us could hold enough pressure on the wound.

"I'll carry you," I said. I bent down in front of her and told her to climb on my back. She managed to keep her legs around my waist all the way to the lab door, then she gave up. I dropped the flashlight and used both hands to lug her all the way up to the third floor.

She was unconscious and only opened her eyes one more time.

And yes, I saw death on her face. Time to move on.

I hoisted her up on the platform where she lay breathing shallowly while I mopped up all the blood from the back door *through the hall, up the stairs and into the tower. I even had to take off my jeans and use them to swab the steps.*

I wasn't positive that she was dead, but I was sure that she wasn't going to feel any more pain. I piled my bloody clothes on top of her chest and stood at the controls in my underwear. The crazy machine blinked the last coordinates in blood red numbers. The date had to be changed. I dialed it back thirty years to 1989. I subtracted ten feet and sent Erica Wills to a junkyard grave directly under the rusty car. And then, with a most iron will, I blocked the whole thing from my memory.

Chapter 18

My mom patted my hand, but my dad sat perfectly still. I looked at him first. Those kind eyes of his held sorrowful regret, as if he himself were responsible for my wrong-doings.

Why wouldn't the ground open up and swallow me when I needed it to?

I cast my eyes to the floor then over to my mom.

"Nothing we can do about that," my mom said, switching from patting my hand to grasping my dad's hand. She looked at him and repeated, "Nothing, Conner. We can't change a thing. We stick to the plan."

My parents had a plan? Mom glanced at the wall clock. "Somebody's going to show up sooner or later. Hurry up, Laken, tell us about the next one."

She took my hand again and the thought occurred to me that she was checking my pulse and temperature. If they knew about all my travels maybe they knew about the side effects I'd suffered and were watching for more. I felt fine though. Well, hungry enough to eat a bear and a little itchy around my neck and waist.

"Laken?"

"Technically the next one was Ciera," I said, "but I'll tell you about Melissa first. That was the younger girl who taunted me along with Erica at Homecoming."

Telling that story wouldn't take as long.

Last summer had been hotter than ever. Most days I'd go to the lab with my parents and then roam around the woods, walk into town, shop a little, dangle my feet in the river, buy ice cream. It was a boring time with no real friends though some days I met a few kids at the park and just hung out.

Melissa walked through the park on the afternoon of the fourth of July. There was a craft show going on with at least thirty white canopied booths taking up most of the grassy area. She was weaving in and out, darting around the displays like she was trying to lose somebody on her trail.

So I followed her.

I wish I hadn't.

She ended up in the park restroom. When she didn't come out after ten minutes I went in.

The pitiful sobbing was enough to break the hardest heart. I instantly forgave her for ruining my one and only Homecoming date.

"What's wrong?" I said. She jerked away to lock herself in a stall. I sweet-talked her for the longest time. Finally she spoke.

"I'm pregnant."

That took my breath away. She probably wasn't even sixteen yet.

"That's not the end of the world." Yeah, easy for me to say. I hadn't been attacked by John yet.

"It's my mom's boyfriend's."

Well, maybe it was the end of the world. The end of this world ... but not a parallel world. I was thinking that a young abused girl could be sent to, say, 1978 when a certain young woman that I'd googled—Shelly Ayers—had started a center for abused girls. Maybe it's a curse to have a brain that thinks in parallel timelines.

"I can one hundred percent help you, Melissa. I know of a place you could go and you can have the baby, give it up for

adoption, and start a new life with no chance of ever running into that man again. No chance."

She came out of the stall then and we hatched a plan. I picked her up at three a.m. in the park and drove her to the lab. I invented the best lie ever and told her she was going to get a medical exam that wouldn't hurt at all. In fact, I told her she wouldn't even remember it. I gave her a slip of paper with the address to Shelly Ayers' help center and told her to hold tight to it. She'd be able to find it in the place—I didn't say past—I was sending her to.

Melissa thought the lab was cool, but felt sorry for the mice. While she sniveled over their cages, I "appropriated" one of the twenty-four-hour sleep agent pills from the drawer. Then we went through the arch and down the hall toward the tower.

She wanted to peek in every cell window. I let her. I stopped on the second floor and had her wait while I grabbed a hundred bucks in old twenties. She didn't have a cent with her. She divided them up into different pockets, an interesting security strategy I thought.

When I switched on the lights in the third-floor tower she visibly shook.

"Want a pill to relax?" I asked, holding out the point two milliliter capsule.

"Sure. I hate doctors. But it's your mom, right? I heard your parents were both doctors." She sucked the pill down.

I nodded. They did have doctorate degrees, but not in medicine.

"Climb up on the table and I'll let her know you're ready, or almost ready, okay?" I tapped on the control screen like it was an intercom system and pretended to call my mom, but really I *was inputting the date, July 5th, 1978, and the coordinates, which I hoped matched the park in town.*

I smiled at Melissa and for one immaculate moment thought what a good thing I was doing. Her pill kicked in then and she laid her head back, closed her eyes, and dropped the paper. I hurried over to the machine and tucked the paper back in her fist. She was out cold and would probably be found fast asleep in the park. Long, long ago.

I double checked the date and coordinates. Then, with a disconcerting satisfaction, I flipped the lever and Melissa vanished.

I finished my tale and drummed my fingers on the kitchen table.

"So," I said, "that about covers it with time traveler number four." I tried for a cute laugh, but it sounded more like a sick cough. "I'm not sure if she made it or if I sent her to a grave like, like Erica and Megan and ..." I really didn't want to mention the guy, but I did, "... and John, the intern."

My parents exchanged looks. They'd have me locked up for sure.

"Don't worry," my mom said, "she made it. She changed her name. Gave up a little girl for adoption. Worked at Shelly Ayers' center for a long time. In fact she may still work there."

I did not in a million years expect her to ignore my confession about John and give me info on Melissa that was so specific and made me feel like I'd done the right thing after all, at least where Melissa was concerned.

"How do you know all that?"

"She'll explain later," my dad said. Those were his first words in half an hour. "It's just a coincidence."

"There are no coincidences," my mom said with her usual curl of the lip. A private moment passed between them, one I'd seen a hundred times, but never gave any thought to before. My parents were hiding something bigger than the time machine and the hibernation pills.

"Tell us about the other two. Numbers three and five. Ciera and Cara? Right? The papers didn't give them much play after their mothers minimized their disappearances as pattern behavior. They'd both run away before."

My dad folded his arms and looked ready to analyze my next revelation.

"Okay," I said. "Well, they were a year ahead of me. When I was in ninth grade and Ciera was in tenth there was this guy in her class, Bryan, who liked me. He was like rock star gorgeous. I wasn't the only one with a crush on him. I was positive he was going to ask me to Homecoming, but Ciera stole him away. You can imagine how. He moved away at the end of the semester, and she ran away for about a month."

In the most carefully chosen words I managed to portray to my folks the nasty, promiscuous girl that was Ciera. Cara, too. They were indisputably the lowest of the low, ugly on the inside in spite of their pretty names, and ugly in their actions. In my opinion they were both on a mission to infect every guy in our school with one STD or another.

"I sent Ciera to 1980 and Cara to 1994. I don't know if they made it. I sent them to the hill behind the pump house. They might be, I mean there's a chance, because of the coordinates, they might be buried there."

My dad started bobbing his head then. "Right. Right. The elevation coordinates change at the whim of the government satellite controllers. Very risky to trust those numbers."

"Honey," my mom said, "we're not angry with you. Everything you've done had to be done. There's right and wrong in all of this, of course, but each of us had good intentions. Not that I'm making excuses …" She glanced at the clock. "Oh! We really need to go, Conner. Empty the safe, including the you-know-what, and let's get ourselves to the lab."

Suddenly it was like a volcano erupted. They both jumped up and so did I. What had just happened? I'd confessed to murder, hadn't I? But my parents were acting like, like it was no big deal.

"You shower and change as fast as you can, Laken. Pick something warm to wear. We'll probably go to January or February."

"What? Why?"

"The police are going to start asking questions. Your dad has already gone back in time and set up new identities for us. And he went forward and set a program to destroy the time machine."

"What? How did he get back? The machine is broken."

My dad stopped halfway down the hall. They both looked at me like I'd set their firstborn on fire. Well, I guess I sort of had.

They stood there stupefied.

I explained. "I jumped forward from last December to today and while I was in the machine there were other trips to the past going on and, I just realized, your trip to the future and back. I think my having the coordinates the same as the platform gummed up the works. There was a scary 'boom' sound and then the machine wouldn't reset."

They still stood there, eyes narrowing, brains evaluating.

Silence.

I added, "I was going to go back for Sky, that's why I had those pills and the money in my pockets." I jerked my thumb toward the money and pills on the table. "So if you went forward and came back using a working machine in the future, then …" I couldn't quite say what I was thinking.

"You can't go back for Sky." My mom's voice measured out the prohibition like a death sentence. "You can't ever go back for her."

She looked hard at my father. "See, Conner? That machine is broken for a reason. She can't go back. No coincidences. We should dismantle it before we move on. There's obviously been a temporal paradox or a causal loop if you managed to get back from the future."

The whole world crashed around me then. History was repeating itself. When she was my age my mother had lost her best friend, the girl she named me after, and now I was losing my best friend—you, Skylar—and my whole life, and maybe my parents if we couldn't use the machine.

It wasn't fair.

Life wasn't fair.

I burst out crying and my mom held me, whispered the obligatory "There, there, honey" and added "I'm your best friend. I'll always be here for you."

When I was done blubbering, I thought to ask why we couldn't just stay. "Why can't we tell Sky's parents I didn't see her this weekend?" I was not above lying if it meant we could stay and work on a way to rescue you. I'd never betray you on purpose.

My mom motioned my dad to come closer.

"Laken," he said, "I've been to the future. I really have. Now maybe I or maybe you created a paradox, uh, a contra-diction of causality, that is … something really dangerous to the fabric of reality. And maybe things will be different, but in the future I visited, well, a number of bodies will be discovered a year from now." His kind eyes bore into mine. "Discovered on our property, Laken. In the woods, under the hill. Some were there for decades so you wouldn't be implicated, but three of them are pretty recent. There's no doubt they'll be connected to you." There was absolutely no judgment in his eyes. "I believe in you, honey. I don't think you meant to hurt anyone. And I'm not even going to ask what happened with John, because I'm sure it was self-defense, but your future will have to be in the past. Understand?"

I did.

Chapter 19

Obediently, I showered. I didn't need much time to clean off twenty-six years of hibernated skin and grime. I was much fresher having endured the hibernation below ground, refrigerated. I layered on the clothing, packed a bag with socks and shoes, jeans and tops, underwear and pajamas.

I crept to my parents' bedroom door and listened to their hushed discussion.

"No, she's not ready to find that out yet. It would be too shocking for her. She's not mature enough," my mother said. I wondered what I'd need to do to be more mature. I was almost eighteen. I understood Novikov's self-consistency theory. They'd left me on my own plenty of times. Heck, Sky, if you added up my years of hibernation, I should have been collecting social security checks. I was plenty mature.

I heard the click of their bedroom safe opening. I knew that was where they kept deeds, birth certificates, money, and the mysterious 'you-know-what' that my mom had mentioned. I inched closer to the door frame hoping to hear more of their quarrel, but my dad yielded to her decision. It was quiet.

I heard muffled movements, then my dad said, "Here. Put it on and keep it under your blouse, out of sight. We'll split up the money and documents and use these travel pouches and the money belt. We still have to go to the lab even if the machine is down. If I can get it to work, no problem. We'll go to 1969 as planned, but if it's broken, like Laken described, well, we'll switch to plan B. I'll delete the software program, we'll collect the hibernation pills, and start gorging ourselves on the protein bars."

My mom sighed and spoke in a normal voice, making it easier for me to listen. "How far into the future do you think we should hibernate?"

That was all I could take of eavesdropping. I knocked before I barged in. My mom turned her collar up and held a hand against her chest. "Laken, what is it?" She looked surprised and guilty. For a second I thought they weren't planning on taking me with them.

"I'm packed and ready."

"Oh, sweetheart, you can't bring anything. We'll buy all we need when we get there."

"What aren't I mature enough to know?"

My dad snorted, pulled on his beard absently and looked ready to tell me. My mom shook her head at him. "It's just some personal stuff, Laken, about me." She dropped her eyes and my dad glanced at the open safe for a second.

"What? Do you have cancer or ...?" I couldn't think of anything worse.

She relieved my suspicion with an honest laugh. "No, nothing like that."

"I worry about that," I confessed. "Sometimes when you take my blood sample, I think you're looking for something in it to save your life. Or dad's."

Their laughter was the teeniest bit too loud and too nervous then. I was on to something, but they weren't going to give in and tell me the truth.

"Let's go," my dad said, putting his hand on mom's back and guiding her past me. I took a step to follow, but as soon as they were out the door I zeroed in on the safe. They forgot to close it and there were still some papers inside.

Four papers.

Two birth certificates and two death certificates. Both birth certificates were for Laken Marie Mitchell, but neither one had my birth date right. One was dated fourteen months before I was born and the other was a year before that. I was confused. The death certificates made it all clear though. The first Laken died when she was one month old. The second Laken died at six months.

It blew my mind. I had sisters, Sky! Sisters I never knew about. We shared the same unique name. They were dead and I wasn't. There was nothing on the papers to tell me why they died, but I knew in my heart it had something to do with blood. My mother's blood. That was her secret. My dad knew I could handle it, knew my curiosity would make me look in the safe that he—oh, what a coincidence—had left open.

I stuffed the papers back in the safe, closed it, and hurried after my parents.

The ride to the lab was quiet. You'd think we were an ordinary family with a sullen teen in the back seat and two adults who didn't want to say anything to set her off. But we were anything except ordinary.

Finally, as we turned onto the long driveway up to the monastery, I asked, "If we have to hibernate, where will we do that? We can't use the pump house if the cops are going to be all over the grounds here digging up bodies." It sounded trite to say that and my heart fluttered with shame.

My parents each gave a nod to the other, neither wanting to answer me. We made it to the front of the monastery before my mom said, "We have a number of places. We've never actually

143

used the pump house. That was just for you … and—" She simply stopped mid-sentence and didn't finish. The pump house was for me. And for you, Sky. The thing was you only used it once.

"What other places? Have you used attics or basements?"

They chuckled at my suggestions.

"You're a smart one," my dad said. He put the car in park, ready to unlock the gate. "No, before my first jump we did a lot of research on houses built in the 1950s. On my first trip back, I bought a few around town that had fallout shelters. I hired a law firm to take care of the yearly taxes and maintenance and gave them enough money to handle things in perpetuity. That means—"

"I know what it means. Where are these houses?"

He reached through the window and unlocked the gate. It swung wide. "Well, you've been living in one of them all your life."

"You're kidding. We have a bomb shelter? No way. I've never seen it."

My mom looked back at me. "We've never been far from you. When we left you alone, sometimes we were hibernating in the basement. It only seemed like a day or two for you, but we'd go back several years, stay for a week or month and then go to one of the other shelters or come home and sleep. There's an entrance behind that old dresser that sits against the windowless wall. I was always afraid you'd discover it and find us, think we were corpses, and panic."

I thought about that for a second. My parents had the most bizarre secrets.

"Where are the other houses?"

"Well, the one we'll use so the police don't discover us is about a mile north of the lab, an easy walk."

I had a creepy thought then. "Is one or both of you sleeping in there now?" A chill went down my legs when I asked it and neither one of them said anything at first. We'd cleared the gate and were rolling to a stop.

"There's always that possibility," my dad said. "But last I checked we're all present and accounted for." He chuckled at his joke, turned off the engine, and opened the door. "Let's see if I can fix that machine or if we'll be heading to the safe house."

Chapter 20

I helped my mom count out capsules and separate them into four containers, one for each of us and one for the leftovers, while my dad went to fuss with his machine.

"What about Reese and Mack?" I asked when we finished. "And the mice?"

My mom looked over at the cages and smiled. "I remember the first time I saw those little guys." She looked back at me and her face took on an impression of wistful regret. "I wanted to let them loose. Free them." She stared at me like I should remember that too. "Come on. We're going to let them go outside." She stood up.

"But they're not wild anymore. How will they survive?"

"Oh, they'll do just fine. Don't worry."

We did it. We let them go. All of them. She used the Hiber-wake spray on the seven sleeping mice with red blotches on their fur that were in the room across from Mack. They followed their colorfully tattooed rodent cousins off through the fence and beyond the pump house. Secretly I hoped they would run all the way to town where school kids would find them and, because they were so tame, the kids would easily catch them and keep them as pets.

"And Reese and Mack?" I asked again.

Mom shook her head. We went inside right as my father came into the lab.

"I did it!"

"You fixed it, Conner? Oh, I'm so relieved."

"Me too." My dad grinned. "Give a dose of that sleep agent to Mack and as soon as he's out we'll send him and the monkey back first, like guinea pigs." He clicked his tongue a couple of times and headed for the washroom.

My mom gave me a little arm-around-the-shoulder squeeze. "It'll all work out, Laken. You're being unbelievably calm about this and we really appreciate that. It's one thing to go back and visit the past and quite another to go back and intend to live there, grow up there without your friends and all. You'll have to be careful what you say and how you act until you learn the culture." She snickered and squeezed me again. "It can have its embarrassing moments. You're in for a most unusual senior year."

She dropped her arm and I shivered. A question was on the tip of my tongue, but I forgot it as soon as she said, "Let's go give a five-day dose to Mack so he'll stay asleep after we arrive. That'll give us time to settle in to 1969 before we figure out what to do with our primate friends."

I got Reese disconnected from all the electrodes that ran to the computer. I cradled her in my arms, still wrapped in the silver blanket, and waited outside Mack's room while my mother coaxed him to eat a mushy banana laced with sleep agent. He was happy to do that; then he wanted to play. Mom sweet-talked him down the hall and up the stairs, but he balked at going to the third floor. No matter how much she cajoled him, he refused to move. When the formula kicked in a few seconds later he succumbed to an unexpected nap and fell face first over my mother's feet.

We heard my dad bounding up the stairs before we saw him. When we did see him, we were shocked.

"You shaved your beard." Mom cried out. "Oh, honey, you look so young."

I was speechless. I'd never seen my father without facial hair. He grinned. And he was handsome. He had dimples. I had no idea that he had such movie star good looks. His eyes shone like gems and that kindness that was always so apparent in his gaze was elevated a hundred percent.

"You remind me of when we first met. My friend Laken had seen you first—"

"—but she never had a chance with me." My dad finished the sentence. I'd heard this story a million times, short as it was. It was pretty much the only thing my dad ever said about my mom's best friend, the one who tragically disappeared, the one I—and two older sisters—were named after.

My stomach lurched and twisted when a sudden brainstorm sprung behind my eyes. "We should find her," I said. "We, or rather just you, Mom, should go back to the last time you saw your best friend and then keep watch over her. Maybe you can stop whatever happened to her from happening. If it was an abduction, or if she ran away, or—"

"Laken, no." The glint in my father's eyes showed compassion and regret, but not hope. "I've been back. I followed her. We can't change what happened … why she left your mom. That would be one alteration too many. And fatal."

My mom didn't say a thing, just clutched at her heart, then she reached to take Reese from me, but I shifted to the side and rocked from foot to foot. Dad picked up Mack and stood there looking at us both, a different gleam in his eyes. I stuck my hand out toward his face and he leaned closer to let me touch his cheek. "I like it," I said. My dad laughed and shifted Mack to his other shoulder.

"I was tired of being as hairy as this ape."

I climbed up the steps with my parents right behind me. My dad didn't even try to whisper as he spoke to my mom.

"We tell her, Emily. As soon as we get to '69, we have to tell her."

I absently rocked Reese in my arms while my dad put Mack on the platform. I eyed the readout on the screen and recognized the coordinates as being the hill where you and I first landed. The top of the hill, that is. I wondered if it wouldn't be a good idea to add a couple of feet just in case.

My dad made that adjustment before I could suggest it so I started toward the machine to lay Reese next to her fellow test subject.

"Wait, Laken, we'll send Mack by himself first." He put in the date and motioned me and my mom to stand behind him. I had a déjà vu moment and then my dad hit the switch and Mack ceased to exist in our time and space.

There were no loud booms or crackling fires. Mack was gone. I gave Reese a final cuddle and laid her out on the empty platform. I fixed the blanket and hooded it around her head like a bonnet. She looked like the ugliest baby ever. I stepped back and watched my dad reset the date and coordinates. For some crazy reason I couldn't watch her disappear so I kept my eyes on the red numbers instead. My eyes blurred for an instant and I swear that at the moment my dad flipped the switch and Reese evaporated the date changed.

"Dad. Did you see that?"

"What?"

"You didn't send her to the same day as Mack. It changed at the last second."

"What?" He scrolled through the readout and gasped. "It wasn't only the date. The coordinates are wrong on both of them."

I was totally unprepared for the hurtful shock of having my father scream at me. "Look what you did! Laken, you ruined everything with your last forward trip." Spit flew from his lips. He visibly shook with fury and for a brief moment I thought he was going to hit me. He raised his arm and sent his fist crashing into the red numbers that flickered the latitude and longitude of what was probably Reese and Mack's grave sites.

"I'm sorry," I yelled back. "I didn't mean to. We still have plan B. You said the machine works in the future. It brought you back so it'll take us to the past."

As quickly as his rage surfaced it skimmed over with icy resolve. "Yes, yes. You're so smart. Plan B. We hibernate for four years and eight months, minus one day. You can figure that out, right, Emily?"

My mom nodded, equally shocked. I wondered if a quick temper had become a side effect of his time-traveling.

"Okay. Let's get all the money from the trunk. All the protein bars, too. There's a bag around here somewhere we can put everything in."

"What about Reese and Mack?" I couldn't keep myself from asking. "Are they going to wake up buried alive?"

"I don't know. I just don't know. That could have happened to us. That's why I did them first. Thank goodness you noticed."

He grabbed me and hugged me hard. I missed the tickle of his beard, but the hug put everything right between us again. Still … there was something not quite right.

"Mack and Reese are somewhere back in time. If they wake up it'll be because they're above ground. If they went under the hill then they would have suffocated in their sleep. They didn't feel a thing. Okay? They actually saved our lives."

"If hibernating again doesn't kill us," I muttered. I wondered if I should tell him about all my side effects.

My dad had one more thing to do before we left the lab. I watched as he headed for the pump house carrying a brick with keys. He pressed it neatly in a niche along the stone foundation.

We didn't take the car. I thought a mile walk on a late Sunday afternoon would be a piece of cake, but it was cool and damp and my mind wouldn't stop replaying my imagined deaths of Reese and Mack. It seemed to take longer than half an hour and by the time we reached the street the safe house was on I'd visualized those chimp and monkey faces with mouths open in silent screams, snouts caked with dirt and blood, and bits of flesh rotting off their hairy bodies. I pictured other bodies, too, not so hairy, more human, but equally innocent despite their sins against me. John. Megan. Erica.

Memories of you shoved their way into my head, too. I thought of a plan, a plan to live as quickly as I could through the tedious decades. I was going to have to bear the empty time until I reached June 15, 1994. I'd never forget that date and I'd go to the restaurant and be there for you. I'd be a forty-three-year-old woman, but I'd be able to give you a place to stay. You'd trust me. I'd prove to you it was me. You'd forgive me. Maybe it had already happened.

I played that scenario out as we reached the driveway for the safe house. Then I thought of a different plan.

"Dad? Do you think you could build another machine so when we live to the '90s we could send Sky back home?"

It sounded incredibly easy to me as I said it, but my dad shook his head and pointed up the driveway. "Let's go around back. The key's hidden behind a brick."

"Why not?" I insisted. He walked ahead of us, a little too fast. "Why not?"

"There'd be a terrible consequence," my mom spoke for him.

"Because I'd see her? Or because I might see myself that day? I'm not worried about that. I saw myself before and nothing broke the world in half."

"Maybe it did and we don't know it yet," my dad said. "Just trust us, Laken. You can't send Skylar home."

"Why do you keep saying that?"

"She changed her name," my dad said, exchanging another weird look with my mom. He unlocked the door and re-hid the key.

"How do you know that?" More uncomfortable looks. "She changed her name to what?"

The door opened and still nobody answered me. "Do you really know or are you just guessing?"

"We know. Here, eat another protein bar."

I took the bar, ripped the paper off, and stomped out into the back yard to eat it. I heard my mother tell my dad to give me a few minutes while they stayed inside. I stared at the back of the house and then at the houses on either side. Next door there were two boys silently watching our argument, their batting practice halted, their thirteen-year-old attentions riveted on me.

These were my last moments in 2020 and I might as well have fun. I waved at them. "Do you need a fielder?"

The taller of the two nodded and I walked over. I started to introduce myself with my real name then altered it on the fly.

152

"Hi, I'm, uh, Lauren." That was the first time I used my new name.

"I'm Austin. He's Carson."

The sun was going to set at 7:03 according to Austin. I didn't know why he was so specific about it. We played catch for half an hour after that, until it was too hard to see. The boys were fun and even though they were a few years younger I had a good time. Carson went home and Austin asked me if I was moving in to the house next door. He could see furniture through the windows, there were lights from time to time, but he never saw anyone.

I told him no and then made up a lie that it had been my grandma's house and she died. We were spending the night and would be gone early in the morning. I hoped to heaven that I wasn't leaving clues to our whereabouts if the police came looking. The kid was smart enough to ask me where our car was. I lied again, said it was already in the garage, and told him goodnight.

I went inside and locked the door behind me. The house was chilly. I wandered around and checked all the rooms, used the bathroom, and stared at my seventeen-year-old self in a hazy mirror. I understood depression then. I saw it in the reflection: I looked lifeless.

The basement stairs were off the kitchen and I clumped down the steps in the dark, found the light switch at the bottom, and switched it on. I think it was a little warmer in the basement than upstairs. There was another glow of light that led me to the hidden bomb shelter. I stood in the doorway and let my gloomy shadow announce me. My parents looked up from the bed they were sitting on together.

"Did you have fun?" my dad asked. He got up and rummaged through the bag for some protein bars.

"It was okay."

"Here, eat some more. Then we'll take our pills."

I wolfed down four bars and drank two bottles of water. I actually wanted to hibernate and get this part of my life over with. It was pretty motivating to know I'd get some answers after we time-traveled. My mom handed me my case of pills and told me she and dad had dibs on the bottom bunks. I'd have to go up a level.

I looked around the shelter. It was roomier than the one under the pump house and must have been designed for a larger family. There were a fifth and sixth bunk so close to the ceiling that you'd have to be a pancake to sleep up there.

"I'm going to check all the doors," my dad said. I didn't bother to tell him I already did.

My mom said she'd go with him. "I need to use the bathroom," she whispered, like it was some shameful secret. She set the other two cases of pills out on the bed before she went.

Alone in the shelter I made myself useful. I grabbed three woolen blankets that were neatly folded and placed one on each of our beds. I opened their pill cases and figured that the one with more pills was for my dad. He had at least fifty pounds on mom and me. I set his case on the first bed and put mom's on the other bed. I kicked off my shoes and climbed up to the bunk above hers. It was tight with that extra bunk over me. I wouldn't be able to sit up without smashing my head on the metal underside.

I lay there and opened my pill box and looked at the various sizes, remembering how you had figured out the formula, how you had awakened a day before Megan and me … and that's when I got the idea to do the same thing. I took out one of the smallest pills and stuck it in my pocket. It was an impulse thing, but I wanted to do a little exploring in my world one last time before I was relegated to the 1960s. I'd get to wake up a day before my folks and check out the future. And really, Sky, I was hoping you'd be in it.

Chapter 21

Time Machine Date: 2024

Who would have thought that the tiny blue light my dad plugged in to an outlet near the door would still be working after four years and eight months, minus two days? But it was, and it gave off enough light for me to get my bearings. The relatively short hibernation apparently left me with no side effects.

I remembered not to sit up right away and knock myself out on the bunk above me. I rolled over and stretched each muscle with ease. My dreams had been punctuated with animal funerals, Skylar rescues, and heavy breathing in the dark. I reached for the ladder on the end and moved myself into the safest position to descend without disturbing my mother.

Her breathing was light and feathery, my father's was heavy like he was having a nightmare. Then I heard another sound, a shallow gasp that I was certain came from the bunk above mine. No longer groggy, a few possibilities raced through my mind. I climbed up instead of down and stretched my hand across the uppermost bunk.

My fingers found long hair and soft cheeks. I drew my hand back so fast I smacked it on the ceiling. Then I pressed my palm against the sleeping face and put my other hand on my own chin and nose to mentally compare the two. It felt like … me. The implications whirred through my head and gave me a problem I'd need to work out in the next twenty-four hours or less.

Was it me? Who else could it be but me? My mom? You?

My heart skipped and my mind spun with the repercussions of a true paradox. I really might be caught in two or three places at once, looping around through time, living in the past and the future.

What I needed was to turn the lights on. I don't know why I didn't think of that first. The light wouldn't wake my folks. I could look through the bag, too, and use the Hiber-wake on whoever was up there.

After scrambling awkwardly down the ladder, I put my hands out in the inky blackness and moved slowly toward the blue light. I explored along the rough surface of the block walls until I found the electrical conduit that ran to a light switch. I flicked it on and took in every inch of the room. My mom's face was so peaceful. My dad's had an inch of beard.

I put my shoes on and stared at that top bunk. The sleeper had to have been there already when we arrived. A prickly wave of foreboding snaked through my senses. Suddenly, in the light, I didn't want to know yet who it was or why she was there. I turned away.

The door was barred, but it was not a problem to unlock it. I had seen my dad pile up a dozen empty boxes to conceal the door, but they were no longer blocking the entrance. Huh, maybe the sleeper came down here after we did. I walked across the basement. There was a light gray filter of morning light seeping in the ground level windows, enough to tell me the outside world had snow.

If mom's calculations were right it was the first week of December in 2024.

The steps creaked and I reached the kitchen which was probably about forty-five degrees. I should have brought the blanket with me.

157

I sneaked around to all the windows and looked out at the winter scene.

Upstairs I used the bathroom, found clothes in the closet and considered taking a shower and changing. The hot water, or rather lack thereof, stopped me cold. Instead, I settled for washing my face with chilly water, no soap, and wiping my bare skin down with a towel soaked in the frigid water. The furnace popped on for all of five seconds, keeping the vacant house from completely freezing.

It was curious that there were clothes and towels and bedspreads, but I supposed that only meant my parents had thought of contingencies. I'd never wear the outdated things that hung in the closet unless my current clothes burned off my body. I shook them out and sniffed them before re-dressing. A single capsule escaped a pocket and I retrieved it, tucked it back in, and pulled on my jeans, shirt, and sweatshirt. There was a bottle of perfume, a fragrance called Shalimar, that looked like it was a hundred years old sitting on the dresser. It still had some potency so I sprayed myself generously.

The sound of a school bus coming around the corner drew my attention. I stood at the upstairs window and watched it slide to a stop. There were only a couple of kids waiting and they took their time boarding. As it pulled away, I remembered the kid that lived next door, or at least he had lived there four and a half years ago—yesterday to me. He'd be my age now.

Glancing over at his house I noticed a number of footprints leading from his backyard over to this house. I went around to all the second story windows and looked down. Obviously, someone had circled the house, stopped at every window and peered in. Those footprints weren't there five minutes ago. The butterflies in my chest flapped down to my stomach and my teeth chattered, not due entirely to the temperature inside.

I hurried down to the first floor intending to go all the way to the fallout shelter to retrieve my blanket, but I stopped cold in the kitchen when I saw a big guy at the back door, his shoulder pressed to the door window, his hand on the knob. I'd left the basement stair light on and the yellow glow played off the window, glinting in his eyes as he turned his head and stared at me.

My muscles didn't move. My shoes were glued to the floor. My mind raced wildly through a dozen parental bits of caution like "don't open the door to strangers," but settled on Mr. Schemanski's scientific wisdom whereby "the observed rate at which time passes for an object depends on the object's velocity relative to the observer." Remember that one? Reciting the phrase in my head anchored me to the floor.

We both stood stock still. Time did not move. I swear I lived a thousand heartbeats, but not a single second.

Then he knocked. I recognized him as soon as time began again. After he knocked, he rattled the door knob, signaled me to open it, and smiled.

All I could think was my breath had to be the most formidable thing in existence. I wished I'd gargled with the Shalimar.

"What do you want?" I said, still not moving, but twitching my toes in those incredibly tightening shoes.

"To help you," he hollered back.

Jade green eyes promised that he was telling the truth and I moved to the door in one quick glide and let him in.

"Man, it's freezing in here." He was so tall. He brushed by me and went straight to the living room where he turned up the temperature on the thermostat.

"What do you think you're doing?"

"Helping. You were going to freeze to death." His grin sparkled almost as much as his eyes. "Boy, you haven't changed at all." He winked then. Like a stupid, cocky brat, he winked at me and said with a twang, "Lauren."

I still didn't move. The furnace made a grumble and the air in the room crawled across my body making me shiver.

"Here," he said, "take my coat."

He put his jacket around my shoulders and I pulled the edges together and backed away until my butt was against the wall.

"You're Austin, aren't you?"

"So you do remember me. Great. I've been watching and waiting for you to return. Your picture was all over the news and the internet the day after I met you."

"Then you know—"

"—that your name is really Laken Mitchell. Yeah, I know. Your picture and that other girl's, Sky something, were all we saw for months. Then the police found all those bodies."

"Please don't tell anyone that we're here."

"I wouldn't do that. I never told anyone about that day we played catch."

I pulled the jacket tighter, nervous then and colder than I was before. I looked down at the floor and tried to formulate the question that I was itching to ask, but I suddenly grew dizzy. I kept my head down and stared at my feet.

My bare feet.

I jerked my head up.

There was no one else in the room with me. No grown-up Austin. No jacket around my shoulders. Just my blanket—that I was sure I'd left downstairs. I wanted to scream myself awake, start over.

I stumbled down the basement steps and hurried to the fallout shelter. The light was on. My shoes were where I'd left them almost five years ago. How was that possible? I hadn't put them on yet?

My parents' faces were serene.

I let the blanket drop to the floor and scurried up the ladder. This time I climbed all the way up and looked at the top bunk. The empty top bunk.

Whoa. I descended, a little dizzy, and looked through the bag for the Hiber-wake spray. I spritzed some in front of my face and then gave my mom a dose.

She woke to hearing me sputtering out my crazy dream. I rambled on about footprints and perfume, tight shoes and the boy next door. She sat up and grabbed my shoulders and pulled me to her chest.

"It's hibernation sickness, Laken. Don't worry. It'll pass. You were hallucinating, that's all—dreaming while you were awake or maybe not fully awake."

She squeezed me tightly and I felt a hard bump at her breast bone. I imagined a chest plate of gold, valuable insurance to pay our way into the future if we couldn't use the time machine.

"So, should we use that stuff on your dad or let him sleep in?" She nodded toward the Hiber-wake spray that I'd dropped to the floor and let roll in his direction.

"We could let him sleep in." I pulled the lone pill from my jeans and confessed. "We're a day early."

She didn't get angry. "Then we'll let him sleep. I don't think there'd be any harm in having a girls-only outing."

Chapter 22

H ave you been to this day before?" I asked. I stood
outside the bathroom and watched my mother rinse her
face while I shivered away the buzz from the hallucination.

"No, but your father has. Just that once that he already told
us about."

She dried her face and hands and then gargled with plain
water, finishing by gulping down handfuls. "I took a few short
hops at first. I didn't much care for the burning sensation. But
going into the past was not at all uncomfortable for me. I've had
some weird hibernation side effects coming back, though.
Swollen tongue. Hallucinations. Deafness. Some rashes." She
smiled at me. "It doesn't last long."

She pulled out the flat travel pouch that was tucked in above
her waist. "I'll move forty dollars to my pocket, so we can buy
some lunch. I'm hungry. How about you?"

"Starving."

"Okay. Let's find some coats in the hall closet."

I had some questions about the safe house and the other ones
they'd set up. It was evident they'd thought of everything. She
explained why there were so many bricks with keys attached. It
wasn't only to keep the interns and me from losing them. There
was one time when they'd gone back twenty years and hadn't
been able to get into a house to hibernate. The law firm handling
the safe houses had changed the locks and the hidden keys were
useless. My dad had eventually broken in, but after that they took
the brick when they time-traveled and that meant always having

an easy way to break a window. The firm would have the insurance company fix it; no one ever found the hidden shelters.

Mom pulled out a neutral-colored pea coat that fit me fine. Hooray, I wouldn't freeze to death walking to town. She threw on a brown trench coat and cinched it at the waist.

"What if someone sees us leaving the house? Will dad be safe?"

"Of course. We'll only be gone a couple hours at most." She put her hand on the front door. "If you act like you belong here, nobody will take notice."

We didn't even lock the front door. We stuck our mitten-less hands in our pockets and walked down the street like we had a purpose. We pointed at Christmas displays and commented on the houses that were decorated. When we got to the main road, I realized how close we were to your subdivision.

"Maybe we should go see Sky's parents," I said. It was an impulsive idea that jumped out of my mouth before I had a chance to reel it in. I thought my mom was going to hyperventilate. "Not a good idea, is it?" She stared at me, her eyes scrunching closer together. "But for them it's been almost five years." She still didn't speak. I rambled on, "So, maybe she did get home. Maybe dad invents another—"

"Laken. Stop." I thought she was going to give me the rest of the lecture about dichotomies, contradictions, and incongruities. But then she didn't. "All right. Let's go see if they're home. Of course, they might be at work. Or maybe they moved away when Sky never returned."

"Or," I said, not noticing that my mom turned the right way before I did, "maybe I'm going to time-travel back to get her tomorrow and she's off to college now."

"Yeah, maybe she's studying to be a veterinarian after all."

163

That comment made me think of Reese and Mack and a surge of sadness came over me. We walked through the slushy snow, our feet getting wetter and colder. We didn't exchange another word until I pointed out your house.

We stopped at the mailbox because my mother noticed it wasn't your last name—Stone—above the address. "They've moved away," she sighed.

"Or died of a broken heart," I said. Too much guilt washed over me and I turned to hug my mom. The tears escaped, dripping off my face like the icicles that were melting on the eaves. My mom's face was wet, too. "I just had a teensy hope that she'd be here. You know?"

"I know, I know. But she'll always be with you … here," she tapped her heart and then her head, "and here." For a moment I thought she had scientifically profound advice to add, but then it was, "Let's go get some food from the grocery store and take it back." She wiped at her face. Then, quite unlike her, she opened the mailbox and pulled out the bills inside. They were addressed to some strangers named Anna and Doug Villaruel.

"Mom. What are you doing?"

"Checking the postmark. Look. This was sent December 2nd and it's delivered already. Your dad wanted us to get to the lab on December 4th, the day before it's set to disintegrate."

"It's the 3rd because I didn't take one of the pills. I woke a day early."

"What if I figured the math wrong when I doled out the pills?" She ran her fingers along her throat, looped an inch of silver chain over her fingernail, then tucked it out of sight.

"The newspaper," I said, grabbing out the daily press. Hardly anyone subscribed to it unless they were eighty years old and couldn't use a computer. What a coincidence that there'd be one in your old box. I ignored the headlines and checked the date. "Oh crap, mom. It's the 4th."

We hurried back to wake my father.

The thing was, my brain started putting a few more clues together as we ran. It was late morning and it probably *was* December 4th. What a coincidence that I had chosen to cut short my hibernation by one day. All my time-traveling had made me smarter while my hibernating had only given me a few physical inconveniences. But what if I had also developed some other inconveniences… gifts … or sensitivities? Because, right then, as my mom linked her arm in mine and we hustled across the street before the light changed, I remembered a similar moment when I was rushing with you across a different street in this town. I'd seen the grown-up Shelly Ayers and then experienced a black out that lasted for most of that day-long trip to '94. I'd written it off to a time-travel side effect. Perhaps there were cross-over aftereffects between the time-traveling and hibernating. Yeah … because I realized I'd just seen an object that triggered a memory … and I was afraid I was going to lose consciousness in the middle of the road. The silver chain my mom had on was—

She dropped my arm at the steps to the front door. I had, in fact, blanked out the last few blocks and forgotten what my unbalanced mind had been reaching for.

We rushed downstairs and, after yelling at my dad and shaking him didn't get him to open his eyes, mom used the Hiber-wake spray.

His first words were curses, which was very unusual for him. I'd heard him swear maybe three times in my whole life. Ever. I wrote it off to hibernation sickness, especially when he

165

immediately jumped up and started brushing imaginary bugs from his arms.

Mom gave him another spritz of the stuff and two seconds later his whole demeanor changed and he was Conner James Mitchell, scientist extraordinaire, again.

"Conner," my mom said. "We have to hurry. It's December fourth. It's still morning, but we don't want to cut it too close."

He gave his left arm a shake and checked his kinetic watch. "Right, right." He scratched at his new short beard and looked at me. "Are you all right, Laken?"

"Sure. And I suppose you should start calling me Lauren— that's the name I've chosen."

"I suppose I can get used to that." He smiled and took my mom's hand. "I got used to it when your mom changed her name for me." He winked at her and my stomach did a flip-flop, followed by another black out.

I came out of it as we stopped by the pump house. I'd walked all the way there keeping my steps in line with their footprints in the snow, seeing only the white impressions and thinking no thoughts at all. All these aftereffects were getting on my nerves. Literally.

My dad pulled the brick out of its nestled spot along the foundation and jangled the keys. "Our luck is holding," he said.

I turned and looked toward the hill, but the contour had changed. Trees had been bull-dozed, the land had been mined of its bodies, and the hill had been refashioned into an array of snowy pits. My first thought was that we'd awakened in a parallel universe. Then I saw the pump house looking exactly the same as ever, its stones dull in the shadow of the monastery-turned-lab.

My mom pulled me away, but I kept looking back. That was the moment I knew I was going to lose my mind completely if this last time jump didn't wipe the slate clean. I needed a total black out or a memory reboot.

There was police tape across the broken lock at the gate and more of the yellow tape at the back door. I was sure we were going to find the place vandalized and the time machine confiscated, but there was no evidence that anyone had gone inside. My dad mumbled brief praise for his law firm and 'getting what you pay for' which did a lot to calm us all down.

The lights worked. Dad made us tip toe in case another version of him was in the tower though he kept shaking his watch and assuring my mom that we were right within the correct window of time. What a coincidence.

We got to the big arched doorway that led to the bedroom hallway when I got one of my time-travel-enhanced ideas. "I need to use the restroom," I said. "I'll come right up to the tower in a minute."

"Meet us in the supply room first."

I used my minute to go to the last place I'd seen John working. That particular work station probably hadn't been used since he 'disappeared.' In the bottom drawer I found a stash of the hibernation pills, neatly disguised as breath mints. They were layered into pocket-sized red and white tins labeled 'made in Great Britain'. He probably had plans to sell them on campus. Jerk. I stacked them across my left forearm and cradled them until I reached the second-floor supply room.

My parents were changing into some pretty awful clothes. I found a black patent leather purse in the sixties section and stuffed the 'breath mints' in it. Mom was wearing a black and white knee length coat with six huge buttons. She held up a brightly printed shift dress and winter coat with fur cuffs and collar.

"Gross, mom. Stick with the one you've got on."

"Oh, but this is for you. Those red boots, too."

I probably wasn't going to like the sixties much, but there was no time to argue. I changed clothes.

Dad had to use the keys to get into the tower. That was the good news. The bad news was that the destruct program he'd uploaded into the time machine on his other visit was ticking down at double speed.

"Is that going to be a problem?"

"I don't think so. You and Laken, uh, Lauren, get on the platform. I'll send you first and then I'll set it for myself. I'll be seconds behind you so roll out of the way fast."

"The hill?" I asked.

"Yes, I think that's still the safest landing point based on the fact that your first send-back, Shelly Ayers, was successfully sent to the sixties. To that spot, right? That time era was before GPS, but the Air Force had a radio navigation system then and the Naval Research Lab launched time navigation satellites in '67. The coordinates should be spot on."

I stroked the patent leather purse, nodded absently as my dad blathered on about migrating orbits and synthesizing technologies, and, with that new mental 'gift' I had, I reviewed my previous conversations with him about Shelly. And I realized a startling fact: He. Knew. Too. Much.

"I don't think I can wait till we arrive in '69 to know those secrets you're keeping from me." It was a stubborn thing to say and even I could detect the whine in my voice.

With a burst of anger my father shoved me toward the machine. I'd forgotten about his sudden time-traveling-induced rages. My mom hopped onto the platform next to me and put her arm protectively around my shoulders. I'd have to wait and ask him again fifty-five years ago … if I could remember that long.

Chapter 23

Time Machine Date: 1969 – 1974

"Laken. Laa-ken."
My mom's voice brought me round. I opened my eyes to the pale blankness of cloudy skies and wet snow flakes. The atmosphere felt undistorted in 1969—sort of like the air was truthful and exactly what it was supposed to be.

Mom told me that I passed out when we landed and slid down the snow-covered hill. Dad did not immediately follow. We huddled under a pine tree whose boughs collected all the sticky white stuff. Ten minutes later, much to our relief, he appeared.

It was not a good day to be outside. We walked, arms around one another, toward the monastery, which didn't reveal a hint of what it was going to become one day. Two friendly, though sour-faced, monks greeted us at the door. We were lost, hungry, and at their mercy for lodging, my father told them. The monks took us in.

I remembered that I had important questions I needed answered but for the first two days we stayed in the monastery I couldn't remember what those questions were, no matter how hard I tried. I'm sorry to say, Skylar, that I didn't even think of you or my plan to rescue you. All my other senses worked fine except for that one aftereffect, a memory lapse. I found the extra hibernation pills in my new-old purse, but I couldn't remember why I thought we'd ever need them again. I didn't mention them to my parents.

I spent most of our short time in the monastery trying to figure out the monks' routines and asking questions to learn if they ever used the pump house. Near as I could tell they didn't.

The third day my dad walked to town and drove back in a brand new 'solar red' Toyota Corolla. I helped carry the cots we had used back to be stored in the pump house. I got chills thinking that the next person to touch them might be me ... with you—that's when I finally thought of you—standing off to the side whispering words which I still couldn't quite remember.

After we thanked the monks and dad made a donation to their benevolent endeavors, we drove down the winding road and straight to the house my dad had rented. It was, unbelievably, the very house I'd already grown up in, but with horrible furnishings, pink tile in the bathroom, and no microwave. Can you believe it?

I complained to my mother that I couldn't live without the microwave. She laughed and said I had to be patient for a couple of years.

She, however, displayed nothing but impatience. She couldn't wait to go shopping. Me, neither. We needed everything.

Since we arrived on the Saturday before Christmas, I didn't have to go to school yet. That was almost present enough. That and the fact that I was only going to have one semester in the original high school that in my day, well, the next century, would be repurposed as a community center. I had missed the end of my junior year and now I was going to start half way through my senior year.

Those two weeks before I enrolled were the most boring of my life. I was tempted to hibernate through them, but instead I watched endless hours of TV shows, a few still in black and white, and listened to radio stations that played nothing but oldies—brand new oldies. I missed the internet, my phone, and so many other things at first, but I got used to the inconveniences as easily as I began to answer to my new name. My Christmas present was a trip to a beauty salon where they put my hair back to its natural medium blond shade. I also got a diary, this diary, and that's when certain memories came rushing back. I dared to start writing the truth, as an apology letter to you.

I started school on January 5, 1970. I had a harder time than I expected finding my way around the three-story behemoth of a building. There were seven sets of staircases; two were up only or down only and the two in the center of the building were designated boys only or girls only, though that rule was broken often. Every girl I met was Patty, Linda, or Mary, and every single one of them wore a dress or a skirt and blouse. They had a dress code right down to their style of shoes which favored 'penny loafers.' The boys looked like young businessmen in collared shirts, tucked in, with names like Bob, John, or Mike. I would have been burned at the stake if I'd told them my name was Laken. Lauren was rare enough. Teachers kept calling me Laura.

On my second day I encountered two potential prospects for my compassionate mission. Yeah, I totally remembered that part of my past. I kept the hibernation pills hidden under my mattress wondering if I couldn't somehow send a few unfortunate souls to the future in order for them to escape family or boyfriend abuse. Naturally the two girls who chided me in the restroom fit my criteria for assistance. Talk about making an embarrassing situation worse—they acted like I couldn't possibly be so dumb as not to know what to do when I unexpectedly got my period. Sanitary options were wildly different than what we had in 2020.

Anyway, their names went on my mental list if I ever considered the need to resurrect my project to send girls to a different century. Always before I had helped those who hurt me, somewhat out of holding a grudge or wanting revenge—coincidentally—though honestly, I was trying to hold the moral high ground.

On my third day as a senior, I sat in fourth hour brooding over the fact that I didn't belong there any more than you belonged where I'd left you. It seemed like karma or something to end up with sort of the same fate as you.

The bell rang, an awful clanging noise that lasted much longer than the gentle tone I grew up hearing, and I pressed my hands against my ears. Bullets of pain shot across the top of my skull. I couldn't stop the tears.

"Are you all right?"

I swiped at my cheeks. The majority of students were out the door and a few kids for the next class had entered. I looked up at this newcomer and didn't even try to hide my surprise. He was a dead ringer for the boy in my hallucination, the one I thought was Austin. Maybe this kid would grow up to be his grandpa. That thought scared the crap out of me.

I didn't know what to do. No words were going to find their way past the lump in my throat. I nodded, not too convincingly, and stood up. He set his books on the desk behind mine and asked the most amazing thing. "Can I walk you to your next class?"

There was no way to quiet my heart. The connection we had was on some other level, an invisible pull that just happened. I found my voice, "Sure." I wondered if this spontaneous attraction was what you had felt for C. J. when you had obsessed over him to the point of jeopardizing our mission. I let this new

173

guy walk beside me down the hallway, and ignored the teeny-tiny doubt that what I felt wasn't real at all.

His name was Jason Preston and he had green eyes and sandy hair. He'd played on the football team and I was so sorry I'd missed that. The five minutes between classes seemed to last for days. He was so … everything … it was, I thought, quite possible that he distorted time and space. At least that was what my heart was telling me. I have to believe that if you find this, Sky, and read all that I've written, that you'll understand.

He didn't have a car, but he walked over to my house that afternoon, in the snow. We talked for hours. Jason's interest in science matched my own and I charmed him with time theories that I personally knew to be true.

My mom asked him to stay for supper and I thought I'd fallen into one of the black and white TV shows I'd grown accustomed to. My pulse spiked every time my dad asked Jason a question and my face, I'm sure, reddened several times during dinner. For certain I went crimson when we found out his middle name was Austin.

Afterwards I gave him a quick tour of our very own fallout shelter and we sat on the bottom bunk and held hands. We had one of those conversations where you don't need words. He kept looking down into my eyes, smiling that slow smile, until finally he kissed me. My heart went into spasms in a big way. His lips were warm and gentle. There was a purity in the moment that compressed our emotions into a bond that went beyond anything I could have described. I knew what I felt and I knew he felt it too so it couldn't be related to any effects of time travel or hibernation. Right, Sky? I just know you'll understand this.

Anyway, we hadn't been alone downstairs for more than fifteen minutes but it was long enough for my dad to get anxious.

He flickered the lights and called down that he could give Jason a lift home if he was ready to go.

Jason hollered back that he would walk, that he didn't live far, but we both got the unspoken message and went upstairs.

Jason thanked my mom for dinner, shook my dad's hand, and whispered the nicest thing in my ear before he left. I had no desire to attempt my homework then, but I had some serious stuff to record in my diary—see above.

I could hear my parents talking in undertones while they cleaned up in the kitchen. As I walked down the hall I caught a couple of words that stunned me and I turned back.

"I heard you," I said. "What was that you said about me and Jason?"

They gave each other that secret look and I lost it. The pain in my head that the sound of the school bell brought on earlier returned and I cried out. My dad scooped me up, carried me into the living room and stretched me out on the sofa.

"What's wrong, Laken?"

I stayed down all of five seconds then sat up and threw the finally-remembered questions in their faces. "Secrets. You have secrets you promised to tell me. Why didn't I know you had other daughters? Why were we all named Laken? Why couldn't I try to rescue Skylar?"

Dad took a chair and mom sat next to me. She unbuttoned her top button and revealed a bit of silver chain.

My whole world stopped, along with my breathing, my heart, my thought processes, and Time itself. She pulled out the pendant on the end of the chain: blown glass, a lake floating in a background of sky.

Despite so much happening, so much time passing, all the hibernation, the side effects, the memory losses, despite all that, it had been only a couple days since I handed that beautiful charm over to you so you could wear it on your date with C.J.

I reached my fingers out and stroked the smooth surface, trying to make sense of the fact that my mother had the exact same pendant.

"Earth to Laken," my mother said so very softly, so very much like you had. "What are you thinking? Is it your turn to wear this again?" She reached for the pendant's clasp. "I suppose that's fair. I've had it now for, oh, a quarter of a century."

But those were your exact words to me after we hibernated. How could she know? I looked in my mom's eyes, I mean really looked, and I finally saw that young girl she had once been.

It all made sense.

"Are you all right?" she asked.

I nodded. (If you're not sitting down, Sky, you better.)

"When you didn't come for me, your dad, he went by C.J. back then, helped me find Shelly Ayers. She understood immediately and got me papers in the name I chose. I picked Emily because I liked your mother. Then Shelly found me a foster home, helped me get into school and later college. It was years before I realized I *was* Emily."

Digesting those facts took a while. We sat in silence, my father biting his lip and my mother fiddling with the pendant's chain in her lap. I stared off into space and connected all the little things, the clues, the signs, the evidence of the truth that had eluded me.

I scrunched my eyes together and tried to voice my tangled thoughts, "You were waiting for someone named Laken to meet you, to meet you as Sky, when she moved here in 2019. But the children you had first would have been too old."

"We were trying to change things."

"You mean you weren't afraid that you'd cease to exist? That you two would never meet?"

"We thought we might be able to live two lives at once."

My dad added, "You know, be in two places at once and then split off into parallel universes. It doesn't always work. Yet. Sometimes you can only exist a limited amount of time in a fixed point in time. But I think—"

"Conner. Shh. This is enough for her to take in right now. Are you all right, honey?"

I couldn't stop the tears from welling up in my eyes. Sky, do you believe this? Please believe it. You, my best friend, are going to be safe. I really *have* known you all my life. You are going to be … my mom. I know, mind-boggling, isn't it? But awesome.

So, I was utterly relieved. That ten-ton burden of having left you by yourself vanished.

I looked from my mom's grim face—your face, Sky—to my dad's serious scowl and a new thought occurred to me. I wondered if these were the parents I'd grown up with or not. There was something unsettling as I scrutinized their faces. Maybe that wasn't going to be your face.

They urged me to go to my room then and rest, with a promise to answer any more questions later. Instinct and habit made me obey.

I crawled into bed and let a riot of divergent thoughts clamber for center stage. I heard their voices off and on as they cried and argued in the other room, heavy fluctuations in their tone shaking my universe. I cried too. I had to talk myself out of some crazy ideas about alternate realities, alternate parents, even alternate souls.

I didn't sleep a wink that night thinking about every facet of my friendship with you and every aspect of our mother-daughter relationship. So many times as I was growing up mom had emphasized that there were no coincidences while my father held the opposite view. I understood them both. I understood their love, too. How they weren't afraid to chance losing each other to the past or the future, because nothing mattered except the present. But what present was I living in? And what present are you living in?

I came to the conclusion that at some point a paradox had definitely occurred. Probably in the pump house. And this might freak you out, Sky, but there are at least two of you and maybe more than two of me. I figured out that as soon as we decided to time travel you, my best ever friend, were non-existent to everyone but me and my dad. I knew it for sure as I remembered every interaction with others: how Mack had reacted to you, how Shelly Ayers ignored you in the restaurant, how Megan didn't see you. It was clear as Bell's theorem.

By morning I knew in my heart that my parents, whether these were my real parents or alternate versions of them, had prepared me for a final time travel. People couldn't change the past if it was their own, and sometimes they couldn't change the future either if it was meant to be.

Was it a coincidence that our town had so many missing kids? Or no coincidence at all that the first boy to go missing left with a girl in her father's red car? I knew so little of that first tale, but I knew that one single, solitary fact.

Was it a coincidence that such a new car was abandoned on a two-track lane on Benedictine property? And destined to rust away?

178

Did they run away so soon after meeting or did they spend every minute together until summer? I didn't have a clue. I couldn't make it happen any more than my parents could try to have children named Laken. It would happen when it happened—if it happened at all. But I was positive that the missing boy was going to be Jason. And I was positive that the red car was in our driveway.

I was sure of one other thing too: the pump house was available for hibernation for the next twenty-four and a half years.

And I had pills enough for two people to sleep about that long.

Sometimes you can see death on someone's face and there's nothing you can do except move on. But sometimes you can see life, love, and the future … and you *have* to move on.

And from the looks on my parents' faces they were afraid of what I was one day destined to choose.

But there was another reality, too. And I was troubled to confront it in the looks they gave me, the things they said, and the way they treated me. If I had to guess, I'd say pieces of their souls were missing. And I wondered if I was missing some of my soul too.

Chapter 24

I kept my theories to myself and tried to live normally from then on. Well, other than to write everything in this diary.

Jason surprised me with his attentiveness. He showed up between classes and walked me to my next class, even carried my books for me. Somehow he managed to race off afterwards and make it on time to history or English or science. I made a lot of friends just because I walked the corridors with him.

I started to really get comfortable in 1970. There was pressure to do well in school, but that was easy since the hours after school weren't crammed full of other obligations. With no lab to spend my afternoons in I found I could do my homework leisurely, spend an hour on the phone with Jason or, amazingly, chat with my new girlfriends.

No one could replace you, of course, even though technically you were still around. But I couldn't think of my mom that way. We adjusted our mother-daughter relationship into an odd bond with strained moments and forgotten promises. I should have been heart-broken by how artificial our connection had become, but I concentrated on Jason instead. So keep that in mind, Sky, if you grow up to have a daughter and she ignores you to focus on boys.

My father didn't seem to dote on us the way he always had before. He worked long hours in a field that had little to do with science. We never talked about the time machine, but I wore the lake and sky pendant every day as a reminder of how things used to be—how they should have been.

Jason was perfect for me. By March we were going steady and I was wearing his class ring. He asked me to the spring formal dance and I was excited to go. I bought a long pink gown like one I'd seen in the supply room of the lab. The fact that an identical lacey pink '70s A-line dress found its way there must have been a fluke—no one in our house used the word coincidence anymore.

So I guess it was another fluke, an accident of chance, that when I went to the beauty salon the day of the dance, that I should be stationed under a hair dryer right across from one of my "victims."

At first I didn't see her face, only the magazine she was reading. It was Vogue and the model on the cover was blurry because a gauze scarf was pulled up to her eyes. Five strands of chunky beads choked her neck below the barely visible smile. I could read the large print fine: "THE PEACHES AND CREAM LOOK THAT MAKES YOU A BEAUTY NOW" but I squinted to make out the next line. Then the magazine dropped flat into the customer's lap and our eyes met. If either of us had a peaches and cream complexion it was overtaken by rosy shock then.

I began to choke as if the beads of time travel were tightening around my throat.

It was Shelly Ayers.

After months of being immersed in my new life and culture I was stunned. I couldn't take my eyes off her face. The noisy hair dryer hugged the two-inch curlers and framed her expression. I had seen her on my first time travel to 1994, an older successful, charitable woman and now here she was—if it really was her—in her mid-twenties, not that much changed from when I put her in the time machine.

If only I'd looked away, she might have thought I only reminded her of someone. After all, for her it had been seven years since we'd seen each other. And I must have changed too—all that time travel and hibernation.

But I didn't look away. I stared at her with knowledge in my eyes.

A full minute passed before she reached for the control dial and shut her dryer off, lifted the hood, and motioned for me to follow her. Another minute and there we were, two former classmates from the twenty-first century, crammed into a one-stall ladies' room, our bristly wet curlers pinned to our scalps and our lips pinned too.

Finally Shelly spoke.

"Thank you. Thank you, Laken." Tears spilled down her cheeks. She grabbed me in a bear hug and in spite of the uncomfortable curlers pressing together I hugged her back. "You saved my life. I can't thank you enough. I don't know how you did it, but I am a thousand times better off here and now."

We pulled back, but kept our hands on each other's elbows. "You're welcome. I'm glad things worked out for you ...will work out for you."

"Can you tell me how you did it?"

"I suppose it can't hurt to tell you now. That lab I took you to belonged to my parents. My dad invented a time machine. Simple as that. But it's broken now."

She gasped at that, but I don't think she had any desire to travel back and I wasn't going to tell her I could get her most of the way back if she wanted to hibernate. I still needed a future Shelly to help you—my mom—through the '90s and I wanted to save those pills for an emergency.

She loosened her grip. "I couldn't figure it out at first. Everything was so different and yet this was my town. I knew the streets. I thought I had gone crazy or was dreaming. I lived in a church basement for a year."

"Wow. How did you make your fortune?"

"What fortune? I wait tables and volunteer at the hospital. Getting my hair done here is a once-a-year splurge."

We dropped our hands then and I guess I must have frowned. She had to make big money so she could open the shelter for abused girls.

"So," she said, half smiling, "you're stuck here now, too? You must have brought a lot of money."

Suddenly I felt uncomfortable revealing any more. A fleeting image of her standing over me at the restaurant troubled my thought process.

"No," I said, "well, maybe my parents brought enough to get started, but they'll make their money investing in things like Pepsi, Coke, McDonald's, you know, like they have a crystal ball on the future." My laugh was pathetic and Shelly didn't return it. "And I think Apple comes out this year." Her eyes widened and I could see the gears turning in her head. "You should invest."

"Oh, Laken," she used my old name again and I didn't bother to tell her I changed it, "what a great idea. You've saved my life again. If there's ever anything I can do for you, you have to tell me. Any favor at all."

"Well, this is going to sound weird, but if you ever see me in a restaurant a long time from now and I haven't aged, just pay my bill and we'll call it even. Oh, and a friend of mine will come to you later that night. Please help her. Her name is Skylar."

"I thought you said the time machine was broken."

"Yeah, well, time machines can really be dangerous and unpredictable. And painful. Anyway, knowing your life is working out, that you're helping other abused kids and all, really eases my conscience."

"Helping other abused kids? I hadn't thought of that. What a great idea. Look, I'm really sorry that we weren't better friends after grade school. I don't know what happened or if I did something wrong, but I want you to know that I always think fondly of you."

"Really? You don't remember?" I should have kept my mouth shut. It didn't matter anymore, but the words escaped before my brain engaged. "I got my first period and you had all the boys make fun of me."

The look on her face was unreal. She really didn't remember. Or maybe she didn't do it. My heart puddled into my toes and I wanted to cry. I thought maybe I was undoing the paradox or creating a new one by telling her how to get rich and who to help.

"My mistake," I said. "Never mind."

Our reunion ended abruptly when someone needed to use the bathroom. We finished our appointments—drying, styling—without any further conversation. She left the salon first but not before giving me a note with her phone number on it. I folded it and put it in my purse, but I threw it away when I got home.

I couldn't stop brooding about time travel and its impossible contradictions the entire time I got ready for the dance. Then Jason arrived and he looked both absurd and handsome in his rented tuxedo.

The dance was a total "blast from the past" in my point of view because of how everyone looked. Most of the guys had long scraggly hair and the girls' hairstyles were big and puffy but sprayed stiff. The music was loud and the dancing frantic, no different than my unforgettable experience with Homecoming. Jason thought I looked gorgeous in my pink fashion statement with white gloves past my elbows and my hair in a big up-do with thick curls cascading down. I used plenty of eye shadow and just the right amount of a popular perfume I bought: Shalimar. The bottle looked like the one in the safe house, minus the coat of dust.

After we danced to music which had become familiar to me, though there were a few older songs I'd never heard before, I excused myself to the restroom. I had a flashback to my own awful encounter with bullies at a dance when I opened the door and heard three snotty voices mocking a poor girl in a yellow print dress. Actually, the dress was beyond ugly. What a hideous design. I knew my face wanted to scrunch up in disgust, but I regained control and began to remove my gloves.

"Leave her alone," I said.

They took one look at my serious face, made some tittering grunts and headed out en masse. Maybe the action of removing my gloves was threatening. I just wanted to wash my hands.

"Thanks," the girl said. She looked mortified.

"Sure."

"You're with Jason, aren't you?"

"Uh huh. You know him?"

She blushed. "He was my first crush. You're really lucky. He's the nicest guy around."

She left the washroom and I thought about what she said: I was lucky. But I was starting to see my life running in circles: meeting Shelly, running into bullies at a dance. I set my gloves on the counter and noticed something terrifying. The skin on my arms was peeling off, exactly like when I woke from hibernation the first time.

I found Jason by the punch bowl and whispered in his ear that I really needed to go home.

"Whatever you say." He flashed the biggest smile and then narrowed his eyes. "Anything wrong?"

I wavered between the truth and a lie. I could have said *"it's a girl thing"* and totally embarrassed him or made up a less humiliating falsehood, but I opted for an embellished truth. I put my arms around him in a big hug and whispered in his ear, "I'm molting. I have a sickness related to time travel and if I don't get out of here right away, I'm going to shed my skin on the dance floor."

That was probably a little too provocative and more twenty-first century sexy than 1970 cute, but Jason hugged me back, kissed my cheek and whispered, "Your wish is my command."

He didn't drive me home, though. I guess he did misinterpret what I said. He headed for that old two-track lane that led up to the back side of the monastery. It was our favorite place to park and make out. He never drove in very far, just out of sight of the main road. It was safe and private and we'd had a good number of heart-to-heart talks there in the months we'd been together.

"So what's really wrong?" he said, dousing the headlights and turning the engine off. "I thought you were having a good time."

Enough light from the nearest gas station filtered through the leafless trees to stripe his profile when he faced me.

"I was. The dance was great. You're great. It's me. There's something about me and my family that you don't know. It would shock you to know."

"Like what? You're really from outer space?"

I almost nodded. I knew he was a devoted Star Trek fan, the TV series that is, which had just finished three seasons. I'd seen some reruns and I thought I could make a comparison. "Well, you know how Captain Kirk is always giving the star date?"

"Yeah."

"And how one episode he says it's star date 4523.3 or something like that and the next week it's star date 3211.7? So they kind of time travel." His smile went sideways. I had him. "I can't really prove it other than to make some predictions that you'd have to wait years to see if I'm right, but my family is from 2020. I was born in 2003." I pushed the door handle enough to make the overhead light come on and I slipped off my left glove first and then my right one.

"Oh, my gosh, you're burned!"

"No, it's okay. The first time I time traveled I went from 2020 to 1994 then to get back we had to hibernate and this is what happened. It's just dead skin. It didn't even happen the second time. This must be some kind of delayed reaction from when we went forward, and then came back here."

"Start at the beginning," Jason said, taking both my hands in his. "NASA put a man on the moon last summer. I'll believe anything."

So I did. I told him everything. Even how I killed the intern.

Chapter 25

April and May were extraordinarily confusing months. Jason believed me. He kept our secret. My skin stopped peeling, but I started having headaches. My mother gave me aspirin and said she couldn't take me to a doctor—a doctor in the '70s wouldn't be able to analyze my blood correctly. I wouldn't have been able to endure it except that Jason came over almost every single day. Being around him made the headaches bearable.

He said he'd rather be with me than try out for the baseball team, plus he was worried about going into the Army since he had a low lottery number. He had to explain the military draft to me and how it was tied to birthdays.

"At least you have a birthday," I said one afternoon at the end of May. "I've missed mine a couple years in a row. Sort of." I got all confused when I thought about it. "Well, my birthday my junior year was a couple weeks away when Skylar and I took the time machine the first time. When I came here with my folks we arrived in December and I started my senior year. I should have had a birthday last month, but my new birth certificate says I'll turn eighteen in June."

Jason took my hand. "We'll have a big party. Double the cake and ice cream. I promise." He gave me one of the softest kisses ever. "And nobody but you and me will know you're technically minus thirty-three."

It was good to laugh. I'd done less and less of that when Jason wasn't around. My dad's temper had increased and my mother stayed in her room more and more. I had an awful premonition that none of us would last much longer. I could feel the day coming when I was going to have to try to get home to the future. My real home. I thought if I could hibernate somewhere, not the pump house, and get to April, 2020, maybe I could stop the first me from ever time traveling at all. It broke my heart to think I'd have to leave Jason.

That day came suddenly, in the middle of the week, a few days before graduation. The headaches stopped. My relationship with Jason had blossomed in five months into the most serious thing in our lives, but it was framed by the uncertainty of our futures. He needed to make a decision regarding the war our country was fighting: enlist, wait to be drafted, or flee to Canada. And I needed to decide whether to break up with him or leave without a word. The decision was dropped in my lap three days before we would have gotten our diplomas.

I walked into the kitchen for dinner, sat down at the table between my silent mom and my angry dad, and then … my parents simply ceased to exist. Right before my eyes. I clutched at the lake and sky pendant around my neck, but that was equally non-existent.

Sky, if you are my mom, or will be some day, please try to figure this out. Figure out what to do so this doesn't happen.

Anyway, I ran around the house like a crazy person, screaming their names and looking everywhere. I could not believe I had seen what I had seen. If it happened to them it would certainly happen to me. I even checked the fallout shelter in case new versions of them were sleeping there.

But I was alone.

One hundred percent alone.

I didn't give myself any time to grieve. I acknowledged the panic, but I felt I needed to act fast. I put some food and drinks in a grocery bag, took the blankets off the beds, gathered all the hibernation pills I'd squirreled away, and tried to think if I was forgetting anything.

Then I remembered the brick. I'd need the key on it to unlock the trap door in the pump house. I'd ask Jason to help me get to my future safely, with the fewest aftereffects. I'd need to sleep in the cool dark chamber below ground and I'd need him to promise to move my sleeping body out of the pump house and then back in on very specific dates in the future. He'd have to be alive to do that so I was hoping to convince him to go to Canada. I could assure him that a future president would give him a pardon for dodging the draft.

But I couldn't find the brick. I almost gave up, thinking that the brick disappeared when my parents did. Then I found it in the car. I couldn't figure out why it would be there, but it didn't matter. Call it another paradox. Or a coincidence. I went back inside and called Jason, told him I'd pick him up in five minutes.

Jason was excited for the adventure. He didn't understand the full implications. He thought he was coming with me to the future. I drove us farther down the two-track lane into the forest; branches slapped the sides of the car while he hummed along to the radio. The song's words seemed garbled to me and I realized that the band was the one whose daughters would form Blue Nine Sistas in my day.

I smiled at Jason. He was happy. I parked the car at the fork in the trail where it would sit and rust through time—a virtual grave marker.

We walked to the hill, Jason carrying all our stuff, and then we crept to the pump house and pushed open the door. He was still with me.

He existed.

I existed.

I unlocked the trap door and he used his lighter to help us see until I pulled the ceiling string. I explained all about time travel again and hibernating and he was on board with it all. We ate and talked and ate some more. We passed some time more pleasantly, making out in the bottom bunk.

He was there.

He was right next to me.

And I couldn't, just couldn't leave him behind. It was impulsive, but I couldn't help it. I divided the stash of hibernation pills into two piles knowing I wouldn't be able to fix my past or my future. I did the math in my head and figured we'd make it to 1994 and then we could wait for the first me to arrive with more pills.

We took the pills, snuggled up, and … slept.

Someone shook me, called me Lauren, not Laken, and, of all things, asked me if I knew what year it was. I couldn't open my eyes, but I sensed that Jason was gone.

I slept again certain that it was a dream or maybe I hallucinated within the dream—wouldn't be the first time.

When I finally woke up for real I was alone but there was a candle burning and a note from Jason telling me he'd hibernated until 1989 and would check on me every day until I woke up. He called me his 'Sleeping Beauty' and he signed it 'your slightly older Prince Charming.'

Muscle tremors pitched me forward and I dry heaved. I'd been so stupid. I'd doled out our pills but forgotten to allow for

Jason's much heavier build. How he must hate me for putting
him in such a lonely time and place. And what if I did the math
wrong? We'd taken every single pill.

I rose and steadied myself and tucked Jason's note in my
pocket. I folded up our blankets, I don't know why, and threw
them on the top bunk. Their little bit of weight gave some swing
to the chains, making the bed sway. I turned on the ceiling light
and blew out the candle. I tucked this diary in the back of my
waistband.

That's when I heard the footsteps above. I remembered the
moment I discovered this shelter: I'd smelled candle wax, seen
the sway of the top bunk, and had the eerie feeling of a third me
haunting the space. If this was that moment then I was back in
2019 and Jason would be way more than slightly older. I lunged
for the light string and hoped I could get myself out of sight
noiselessly.

The trapdoor eased open. A man with a brick filled the
opening.

He had a flashlight and he climbed down quickly, calling my
new name and then my old name. It was Jason.

"Over here."

I found the string and fell into his arms. He didn't feel any
different.

"What year is it?" I asked.

"Is that my greeting after I've waited all these years for you
to finish napping? Kiss me." His arms were hard and strong.

I kissed him, and it was wonderful. Joyous. Sweet.

"I still want to know what year it is."

"1994."

"Oh, crap," I tensed up right away. "It's not, by any ridiculous coincidence, June 15th, is it?"

"Nope, it's still May, for one more day. And you're not going to believe how cool the future is."

I laughed at that. I was just happy to have a future. For now. It was incredible that Jason had stayed loyal to me for five years, vigilantly watching over me.

"So, can we get out of this hole?" I asked. "Where are you living?"

"I got a lot of help from a lady named Ms. Ayers. She got me a great job and I'm going to college part-time. They don't make you join the army anymore. You were right about a lot of stuff. To be honest, a tiny part of me thought we were making a suicide pact that day, but mostly I believed you."

He hugged me again. "Life is good, Laken. But it's been lonely waiting for you."

He switched his flashlight back on and pulled the ceiling light's string to turn off the old yellow bulb. He took my hand, led me to the ladder, and helped me go up first.

I paused at the top and glanced around the pump house. I had no more sleeping pills and the invention of dad's time machine was a lifetime away. I was pretty sure I was done with time-traveling. I had an awesome boyfriend and because of him I knew what you, Sky, experienced the moment you met my dad and why you wanted to live in the past. But if you still existed here, in my new universe, I thought I'd better stay away from you.

I did think, though, that I might visit the pump house once in a while—after June 15—just to make sure everyone was tucked in nice and tight and to hide this diary in your bag. It raced through my mind that in two weeks' time the first you would be here with the first me pulling down the cots and getting ready for the initial hibernation. We could still get those pills and finish the journey. Better not though, that would mess things up too much.

I stepped up out of the fallout shelter and waited for Jason to close the trapdoor. The lock clicked and I noticed his hands were empty of the brick and keys. He'd left them locked below. The impossible implication froze my heart, but only for an instant, until I looked into his jade green eyes and the fear for my future melted.

I was a bit more prepared then for the brain-numbing shock I got when we emerged from the pump house into my very own and totally obvious paradox. The sun had bleached the color out of every blade of grass, the tree trunks, the leaves, even the sky.

"I'm parked on the drive," Jason said.

We walked toward the monastery

But there was no gate.

No well.

No arched doorways.

Just piles of bricks and stones, shards of glass and splintered beams, heaped along a gray foundation, with stiffened debris wedged into crevices. I huddled next to Jason and moved slowly, like the ghost I was afraid I was, past a completely demolished monastery.

I shuddered, stopped, held Jason's hand with my fiercest grip and sucked back the scream that was ready to rip through my throat.

Anybody who time-traveled like I did would eventually kill someone, would eventually destroy everything around them. Accidentally or not. Sometimes you can see death on someone's face or in the mirror or in a pile of rubble and there's nothing you can do except move on.

I looked up and found something, forgiveness maybe, in those greenest of eyes. Sometimes you can see a new life right in front of you and you have to forget the old—the destroyed—and move on. I'm an ordinary time traveler now. And this isn't the end.

I asked Jason to give me ten minutes and I ran back to the pump house, finished writing these last few paragraphs, and said goodbye to all my pasts and to you. Now I'll leave this diary here. If you find this, Sky, you can write the ending.

The End

Please don't forget to leave a review on Amazon.

BOOKS by Debra Chapoton

Young adult to Adult:

EDGE OF ESCAPE Innocent adoration escalates to stalking and abduction in this psychological thriller. SOMMERFALLE is the German version of EDGE OF ESCAPE

THE GUARDIAN'S DIARY Jedidiah, a 17-year-old champion skateboarder with a defect he's been hiding all of his life, must risk exposure to rescue a girl that's gone missing.

SHELTERED Ben, a high school junior, has found a unique way to help homeless teens, but he must first bring the group together to fight against supernatural forces.

A SOUL'S KISS When a tragic accident leaves Jessica comatose, her spirit escapes her body. Navigating a supernatural realm is tough, but being half dead has its advantages. Like getting into people's thoughts. Like taking over someone's body. Like experiencing romance on a whole new plane - literally.

EXODIA By 2093 American life is a strange mix of failing technologies, psychic predictions, and radiation induced abilities. Tattoos are mandatory to differentiate two classes, privileged and slave. Dalton Battista fears that his fading tattoo is a deadly omen. He's either the heir of the brutal tyrant of the new capital city, Exodia or he's its prophesied redeemer.

OUT OF EXODIA In this sequel to EXODIA, Dalton Battista takes on his prophesied identity as Bram O'Shea. When this psychic teen leads a city of 21st century American survivalists out from under an oppressive regime, he puts the escape plan at risk by trusting the mysterious god-like David Ronel.

THE GIRL IN THE TIME MACHINE A desperate teen with a faulty time machine. What could go wrong? 17-year-old Laken is torn between revenge and righting a wrong. SciFi suspense.

THE TIME BENDER A stolen kiss could put the universe at risk. Selina doesn't think Marcum's spaceship is anything more than one heck of a science project … until he takes her to the moon and back.

THE TIME PACER Alex discovered he was half-alien right after he learned how to manipulate time. Now he has to fight the star cannibals, fly a space ship, work on his relationship with Selina, and stay clear of Coreg, full-blooded alien rival and possible galactic traitor. Once they reach their ancestral planet all three are plunged into a society where schooling is more than indoctrination

THE TIME STOPPER Young recruit Marcum learns battle-craft, infiltration and multiple languages at the Interstellar Combat Academy. He and his arch rival Coreg jeopardize their futures by exceeding the space travel limits and flying to Earth in search of a time-bender. They find Selina whose ability to slow the passage of time will be invaluable in fighting other aliens. But Marcum loses his heart to her and when Coreg takes her twenty light years away he remains on Earth in order to develop a far greater talent than time-bending. Now he's ready to return home and get the girl.

THE TIME ENDER Selina Langston is confused about recurring feelings for the wrong guy/alien. She's pretty sure Alex is her soulmate and Coreg should not be trusted at all. But Marcum … well, when he returns to Klaqin and rescues her she begins to see him in a different light.

TO DIE UPON A KISS Several teenagers' lives intertwine during one eventful week full of love, betrayal and murder in this futuristic, gender-swapped retelling of Shakespeare's Othello.

HERE WITHOUT A TRACE Hailey and Logan enter a parallel world through hypnosis in order to rescue a girl gone missing.

LOVE CONTAINED After one of the Winston twins dies, the surviving brother loses his faith, ignores God's plan, but never forgets the girl both of them loved. When he returns to the mission field six years later, mysterious things happen. What's a coincidence and what's God's plan?

Coming 2021: SPELL OF THE SHADOW DRAGON

Non-fiction:

HOW TO BLEND FAMILIES This guide gives step by step advice from experienced educators and also provides several fill-in worksheets to help you resolve family relationships, deal with discipline, navigate the financials, and create a balanced family with happy people.

BUILDING BIG PINE LODGE A journal of our experiences building a full log home

CROSSING THE SCRIPTURES A Bible Study supplement for studying each of the 66 books of the Old and New Testaments as they relate to the 22 Hebrew letters.

300 PLUS TEACHER HACKS and TIPS A guide for teachers at all levels of experience with hacks, tricks, and tips to help you get and give the most out of teaching.

HOW TO HELP YOUR CHILD SUCCEED IN SCHOOL A guide for parents to motivate, encourage and propel their kids to the head of the class. Includes proven strategies and tips from teachers.

HOW TO TEACH A FOREIGN LANGUAGE Tips, advice, and resources for foreign language teachers and student teachers.

BRAIN POWER PUZZLES Volume 1

Stretch yourself by solving anagrams, word searches, cryptograms, mazes, math puzzles, Sudoku, crosswords, daisy puzzles, boggle boards, pictograms, riddles, and more in these entertaining puzzles books.

BRAIN POWER PUZZLES Volume 2

BRAIN POWER PUZZLES Volume 3

BRAIN POWER PUZZLES Volume 4

BRAIN POWER PUZZLES Volume 5 (Spanish Student Edition)

BRAIN POWER PUZZLES Volume 6 (Math Edition)

BRAIN POWER PUZZLES Volume 7

BRAIN POWER PUZZLES Volume 8 (Bible Theme)

BRAIN POWER PUZZLES Volume 9

BRAIN POWER PUZZLES Volume 10 (Christmas Edition)

BRAIN POWER PUZZLES Volume 11 (Word Search Challenge)

Children's books:

THE SECRET IN THE HIDDEN CAVE 12-year-old Missy Stark and her new friend Kevin Jackson discover dangerous secrets when they explore the old lodge, the woods, the cemetery, and the dark caves beneath the lake. They must solve the riddles and follow the clues to save the old lodge from destruction.

MYSTERY'S GRAVE After Missy and Kevin solved THE SECRET IN THE HIDDEN CAVE, they thought the rest of the summer at Big Pine Lodge would be normal. But there are plenty of surprises awaiting them in the woods, the caves, the stables, the attic and the cemetery. Two new families arrive and one family isn't human.

BULLIES AND BEARS In their latest adventure at Big Pine Lodge, Missy and Kevin discover more secrets in the caves, the attic, the cemetery and the settlers' ruins. They have to stay one step ahead of four teenage bullies, too, as well as three hungry bears. This summer's escapades become more and more challenging for these two twelve-year-olds. How will they make it through another week?

A TICK IN TIME 12-year-old Tommy MacArthur plunges into another dimension thanks to a magical grandfather clock. Now he must find his way through a strange land, avoid the danger lurking around every corner, and get back home. When he succeeds, he dares his new friend Noelle to return with him, but who and what follows them back means more trouble and more adventure.

BIGFOOT DAY, NINJA NIGHT When 12-year-old Anna skips the school fair to explore the woods with Callie, Sydney, Austin, and Natalie, they find evidence of Bigfoot. No way! It looks like his tracks are following them. But that's not the worst part. And neither is stumbling upon Bigfoot's shelter. The worst part is they get separated and now they can't find Callie or the path that leads back to the school.

In the second story Luke and his brother, Nick, go on a boys only camping trip, but things get weird and scary very quickly. Is there a ninja in the woods with them? Mysterious things happen as day turns into night.

THE TUNNEL SERIES 12-year-old Nick escapes from a reformatory but gets side-tracked traveling through multiple tunnels, each with a strange destination. He must find his way home despite barriers like invisibility. When he teams up with Samantha they begin to uncover the secret to all the tunnels. (6 books in series)

For updates on new releases join my newsletter at
http://www.bigpinelodgebooks.com

Made in the USA
Monee, IL
14 October 2021